Cannons of the Comstock

**Center Point
Large Print**

**This Large Print Book carries the
Seal of Approval of N.A.V.H.**

ॐ श्री गणेशाय नमः

Cannons of the Comstock

Brock and Bodie Thoene

Center Point Publishing
Thorndike, Maine

EVERYTHING IS JAKE!

This Center Point Large Print edition
is published in the year 2002 by arrangement with
Bethany House Publishers.

The text of this Large Print edition is unabridged. In other
aspects, this book may vary from the original edition. Printed in
Thailand. Set in 16-point Times New Roman type by
Bill Coskrey and Gary Socquet.

ISBN 1-58547-182-8

Library of Congress Cataloging-in-Publication Data.

Thoene, Brock, 1952-
    Cannons of the Comstock / Brock and Bodie Thoene.--Center Point large print ed.
    p. cm.
    ISBN 1-58547-182-8 (lib. bdg. : alk. paper)
    1. United States--History--Civil War, 1861-1865--Fiction. 2. Sierra Nevada (Calif. and
Nev.)--Fiction. 3. Comstock Lode (Nev.)--Fiction. 4. California--Fiction. 5. Large type
books. I. Thoene, Bodie, 1951- II. Title.

PS3570.H463 C36 2002
813'.54--dc21

                                                                        2002019133

CHAPTER 1

The clatter of hooves on the rust-colored cobblestones rang like musket fire down the lanes of Richmond, Virginia. As soon as one dispatch rider passed the bronze statue of George Washington, the staccato echo of another's approach could be heard in the distance.

Though they were official couriers charged with bearing military communiqués to the Confederate cabinet, the messengers could not help shouting their reports to the eager citizens who jammed the sidewalks. "The *Cumberland* has been rammed and is sinking!" cried one.

The crowds applauded and yelled their approval. "Hurrah for the *Virginia*! No Yankee blockade shall hold!"

Another rider cantered by.

"What news?" the mob demanded.

"Our iron-hulled alligator has blasted the *Congress* to kingdom come and is turning toward the *Minnesota*," the hoarse-voiced officer croaked.

Directly in front of Washington's statue, the rough, flushed face of Colonel James turned away from the excitement of the street to lock eyes with a small black child perched atop the eight-foot-high block of marble. "You, Mont! Nigger! Look sharp," he demanded. "Don't forget why you're up there, or I'll whup your worthless hide clean off!"

The boy's vantage point on the statue's pedestal lifted him above the heads of the crowd, but he paid no attention to their enthusiasm. The florid-cheeked colonel did not need to remind Mont of his assignment or the merciless temper behind the whip. The child was so intent that he did not even turn his head as yet another dispatch rider galloped past, bearing more news of the great naval battle taking place at Hampton Roads.

The sharp-eyed boy spotted the approaching carriage when it was still a full three blocks away. He could pick it out from all the other traffic on the Richmond street because of its unmatched team of horses. The near horse was a gray, while the off horse was deep chestnut. In an era when respectable gentlemen prided themselves on the perfection of their teams, the object of Mont's search stood out like the wispy beard of President Jefferson Davis.

"He's a comin' yonder," called out Mont in a high treble.

"'Bout time," grunted Colonel James. "All right, shinney on down here right now."

Mont jumped down from his perch and took his position behind his master as the carriage came to a stop.

The young man who stepped from the carriage was clean shaven. He was not wearing a uniform as Mont had expected, but instead wore a brown suitcoat with a dark brown velveteen collar. The knot of his cravat was crooked, and his movements seemed anxious and hurried. He clutched a scuffed leather portfolio against his chest with both hands and peered nervously up and down the street.

Colonel James made his customary approach. "I'm James," he announced with a squinted eye, "and your name is Hastings."

"Avery Hastings," agreed the newcomer. He extended his right hand, but James ignored it, and Hastings awkwardly brushed it against the leather pouch. "How soon can you get me in to see him?" he asked abruptly.

"Depends," remarked James in a stone-cold voice. "President Davis is a very busy man." The two started to cross the street with Mont trailing along behind. "He don't have time to bother with every crackpot schemer that comes around." The distant patter of an approaching troop of cavalry could be heard from the far end of the avenue.

"Crackpot! Schemer!" bristled Hastings, stopping in his tracks and turning to face his accuser. "Colonel," he corrected in an intense whisper, "I'll have you know that it's in my power to deliver California and *all* its gold into the hands of the Confederacy!"

Colonel James remained unmoved and only returned a silent stare.

Hastings quickly yielded to the silence and asked, "Where is my valise?"

"Boy!" James bellowed at Mont. "Fetch the man's bag and be quick about it." He gave Mont a shove that sent the child sprawling on the cobblestones. "Run, blast you!"

Mont jumped up and dashed back across the road in a flurry of eagerness to please. His dark eyes were serious, and he bit his lower lip as his skinny arms strained to wrest the heavy carpetbag from the carriage.

James and Hastings had turned away from the street to enter an office building, but not before Mont caught an impatient glare that made him redouble his efforts.

Raising himself on his tiptoes as he balanced on the carriage's running board, he mustered all his strength to hoist the case upward.

As this last effort freed the valise, Mont jumped backward into the middle of the boulevard without having paid any heed to the cavalry unit now bearing down on him less than fifty feet away. Mont suddenly felt the impending danger of the thunderous noise of hoofbeats penetrate his attention.

Transfixed at the sight of twenty-five riders racing toward him, Mont saw a solid wave of angry-eyed bay war horses that stretched from curb to curb. The ringing of their hooves vibrated through him from the crown of his tightly curled hair to the worn-out soles of his cheap shoes.

The front rank reached him, seemingly a single beast with twenty-four flailing limbs and twelve blasting nostrils. No individual sounds could be distinguished. All he heard was a continuous roll of hoofbeats, shouts and snorts. Mont could not even hear his own scream of terror as the foaming wave crested above him.

Mont awoke with the cry stuck in his throat as the vivid sight of the Confederate cavalry troop replayed once more in his memory. Above the narrow bunk he shared with Nathan Dawson, gingham curtains at the window tossed on a swirl of frosty January air. Sheets and down comforters were damp with the sweat brought on by Mont's recurring nightmare. His heart still drummed in his ears like the echoing hoofbeats of the horses that had borne down on him that long-ago hot afternoon in Richmond. *Was it only his heart he was hearing? Or was it something else?*

A distant rumble of galloping horses seemed to float past the curtains. He covered his face with his hands to shut out the sound and the memory. But the drumming did not diminish. He sat up in bed and stared, trembling, toward the half-open door. If only he could escape the horror of the room—away from the sound . . . away from the dream that would not leave him alone. But his shaking legs refused to move, just as they had stood like wooden posts when the wall of horses had thundered toward him.

He squeezed his eyes tight and forced himself to remember how the brown-suited man had suddenly appeared out of nowhere and propelled him to safety.

A split second more and they would have perished. There had been no attempt to pull back on the stampeding horses. In that frantic moment, Mont had dropped the valise. The bag and its contents had been trampled into unrecognizable scraps of leather and tiny fluttering bits of ragged cloth before those churning hooves disappeared around the corner. Mont had stared in disbelief at the wreckage. It might have been his own body in pieces on the street.

Mortified at Mont's stupidity, Colonel James had sworn to make the boy pay dearly for this public shame. He said it would have served Mont right if he had been trampled. The colonel had whipped the boy with a razor strop every day for several weeks after the incident. But Mont never dreamed about the sting of leather on his bare backside. He only relived the vision of those approaching horses.

Tonight he could not escape the nightmare. He was awake. At least he *thought* he was awake. This was California, not Richmond. His brutal master was long since dead. Mont now lived at the ranch of the widow Dawson with her two sons, Jed and Nathan. Eight-year-old Nathan was snoring soundly beside him. Why, then, could he still hear the sound that carried his mind back to that violent Richmond street?

Another gust of wind off the Sierras carried the rattle of iron shoes on ice-hardened dirt lanes. *Still dreaming?*

He reached out a finger in the darkness and poked Nathan as yet another shudder of fear coursed through his thin body.

"Huh?" Nathan responded sleepily. "Wha . . . Mont?"

"I hears h-hawses," Mont stuttered.

"You're dreamin' agin," Nathan moaned unhappily.

The ghostly drumming rose and fell. This was *no dream!* Now Nathan heard it too and lay silently listening for a moment.

"Hear dat?" Mont whispered.

"Uh-huh." Now Nathan sat up beside Mont and scrambled to the window. Ducking beneath the curtain, he squinted out across the dark yard toward the barn. Mont squeezed in beside him, greatly comforted that the hoofbeats were not merely in his mind, and that his legs were working again.

The tiny orange flare of a match erupted behind the window of the lean-to where Nathan's uncle, Tom Dawson, lived beside the barn. Then the light became brighter as Tom lit the kerosene lamp.

"Uncle is up," Nathan said reassuringly. "Ain't no ghosts we're hearin', I guess."

From the lower bunk, Jed called out, "Go to sleep or I'm tellin' Ma . . ."

Mont did not take his eyes from the back-lit figure of Tom Dawson as the big man wrapped a blanket around his shoulders and stood beside the lamp to listen. Craggy, sunbrowned features displayed concern. Tom reached down to grasp his carbine and put it by the door. Then Mont could see him tug on his trousers and his boots. The sound of approaching horses grew louder.

"Comin' this way," Nathan muttered.

By now the increasing noise of hoofbeats had stirred Jed to a wakeful apprehension. "What is it?" He pulled his comforter tight around him and climbed up to join Mont and Nathan at the window. At the sight of his uncle emerging from the lean-to with rifle in hand, Jed added, "Call Ma!"

A gray swirl of morning fog hung at streetlamp height above the intersection of Montgomery and California streets. The bustling activity of San Francisco's business district had not yet begun. A solitary pedestrian paused in the shadows in the middle of the block, beyond the reach of the lamplight. In unhurried fashion, he extracted a cigar from his waistcoat pocket and lit it. Ducking his head toward the match cupped in his hands, he took the opportunity to scan the sidewalks. Satisfied that no one was following him, he walked briskly toward an even deeper gathering of darkness and plunged quickly into it.

One knock thumped on the alley doorway leading into the building of the Atlantic and European Express Company. After a pause, two knocks followed, then another pause and one more.

A gravelly voice from within demanded, "What is it?"

"An inquiry about shipping" was the short reply.

"Why so early?" The voice from the interior of the building sounded gruff and irritated.

"It is never too early for important business" was the precisely spoken response, every word distinct.

There was a rasping noise as a heavy bar was lifted inside, followed by the sound of two iron bolts being drawn.

"Come in slowly, friend," the whiskey-roughened voice instructed. "And don't do nothin' fancy."

The man with the cigar nudged the door open with his foot and slowly advanced into the spotlight of a bull's-eye lantern that shown directly into his face, blinding him. He carefully held both hands open in front of his expensively tailored coat. When he had moved to the center of the dingy room, he saw that the lantern hung from the bannister of a dilapidated wooden staircase leading upward. The door quickly closed behind him, and the bolts clanked back into place.

"Up the stairs," he was told.

Halfway up, it struck him that he had never seen the form, much less the face, of the doorkeeper. "Very impressive," he muttered to himself through teeth clenched around the smoldering cigar.

Emily Dawson's room was below the loft where Mont

and her sons were sleeping. But it was not the noise of the approaching horsemen that awakened her—she had roused before first light to stir up the fire. The new day promised to be fair and clear-skied, but the feeble light of the winter dawn would be a long time warming the air.

The rocky battlement known as Shadow Ridge curled down among the foothills of the Sierra Nevadas into as pretty an oak-trimmed valley as existed anywhere in the world. Three thousand feet above the level of the Pacific Ocean which lay one hundred and fifty miles or so to the west, the Dawson ranch sat safely above the malarial fogs of the Great Central Valley, but lower than the red-wood-studded backbone of the Sierras. The high passes were shrouded now with snow and would be uncrossable till spring, but in the watershed of the Poso, life went on.

Emily's husband Jesse had located well, and had made a good life of farming potatoes and breaking horses. The Union army had proved a ready customer for both.

At first the war between the States had been only a distant source of unhappy news, until a Confederate conspiracy reached California and engulfed the Dawson home. Jesse and his brother Tom had been close to uncovering the secrets of Shadow Ridge when Jesse was tragically murdered.

Listening to the hoofbeats, Emily paused as she ran a brush through her honey-blonde hair. Her fair complexion was smooth, but a deep sadness lingered in the depths of her blue eyes. Like Mont, she also noted when the approaching riders turned to cross the creek.

Drawing her dark blue dressing gown tightly around her, Emily looked for a shawl to throw over her shoulders. Best see that her brother-in-law Tom was awake.

Shadow Ridge was still thick with Southern sympathizers.

As battles raged in the East, tempers flared higher here in the West. Why would riders come to the ranch at this hour unless they meant to settle some old score?

CHAPTER 2

As his apprehension mounted with the approaching riders, Tom Dawson levered a round into the fifteen-shot Henry rifle he carried. The cold of the brass receiver was enough to make his hand ache, but he took no notice. Five purposeful strides across the yard and he reached up to knock on the door of the house.

"Em!" he called. "Wake up, Emily. Riders coming!"

The door opened at the first knock and Emily stood regarding him, a worried frown printed across her delicate features. "I heard them too," she said worriedly. "What do you suppose it is?"

"More'n likely nothing fretful. But it's a sight too early and icy for this to be a social call. You and the boys stay inside with the door bolted till we see."

"Aren't you coming inside?" she asked, concerned.

"No, I'll be just across the way there." He jerked his thumb over his shoulder toward the corral. "Get Jed to watch the creek side of the place in case someone sneaks up that way, and you—"

"I'll be right here beside the window," she vowed coolly, pulling a twelve-gauge double-barrelled Thomas shotgun into view.

"Good girl," Tom said with a grin. "You just keep out of sight, and if need be," he paused to nudge her shotgun's barrel, "let 'buck' do the talking for you."

Taking his position, Tom stood in the angle formed by the corral fence and the wall of the barn. From there he had a clear field of fire without shooting toward the house, and a line of retreat into the barn if he needed one.

He went through the preparations for battle with a mechanical detachment, loading the Henry's tube magazine and checking the Colt Navy revolver. All the time his conscious mind was racing through a series of questions. Who could be coming? There were gangs of men calling themselves Southern sympathizers, but who really were only thieves and murderers of the lowest sort. There had been raids by Confederate regulars into New Mexico and Arizona as well as the threat that they would rush into California.

Tom's last gun battle with one such outlaw came swiftly to mind. The ache in Tom's right hand was a constant reminder of that fight. Byrd Guidett was buried, unmarked and unmourned, in the pauper's corner of Oak Grove Cemetery, but who knew the whereabouts of the other outlaws with whom he rode?

Tom crouched lower than the top rail and peered over the second whip-sawn two-by-twelve. Where he had placed himself gave him some advantage, but it wasn't perfect. Looking east as he was, the riders would be coming toward him out of the morning sun, which was just now climbing over Greenhorn Mountain.

Sounds like five or six riders coming, he thought. *Not good odds if they're hostile. 'Course,* he reassured himself, *this isn't exactly a sneak attack either*.

The approaching riders turned the last corner off the road and onto the lane leading up to the Dawson ranch. The jingle of harness rings now joined the rhythmically snorting breath of the horses. From the barn, Tom's own favorite mount, Duncan, bugled a warning.

They finally moved into his lane of sight, a moving mass of dark-garbed men on muscled bays. Puffs of vapor from the horses' nostrils streamed back along the trail, as if tracing the passage of a steam locomotive. Brass buttons glinted on the men's caps and shoulders. Sunlight flashed on carbines slung over shoulders. Military men, for certain—but, against the morning's glare, what color coats did they wear? Blue or gray?

A tall, broad-shouldered figure rode at the head of the column of twos. He was flanked by a much shorter man dressed in lighter-colored clothing than the rest. The smaller man seemed to be haranguing the larger, who ignored him.

They clattered into the yard. The horses milled about and called out to those in the barn.

"Hello the house," called out the leader of the troop in a resonant bass voice. A reedy echo from the smaller man repeated the phrase. The two sat their horses nearest the door and were ringed by a semi-circle of four others dressed in the dark blue uniforms of the United States Cavalry.

Tom blew a sigh of relief and eased his grip on the carbine. He stepped up on the bottom rail of the fence and casually swung the Henry across his arm. "Morning, Colonel," he called. "What brings you and Deputy Pettibone out here so early?"

The worn stairs in the warehouse of the Atlantic and European Express Company swayed under the weight of the cigar-smoking man. He passed two landings with branching walkways leading into dusty storerooms, then the rickety treads made an abrupt turn and zigged back the other direction.

He knew he was being watched. He could almost feel the eyes peering at him from the dark shadows. The man smiled to himself because anyone trying to observe him would be able to track only the glowing tip of his cigar on the darkness-shrouded stairway.

A faint illumination suddenly appeared above him at last. The rectangular outline of a curtained doorway loomed above him, showing a rim of lantern-light from a room beyond.

The man straightened his necktie and tile hat, then brushed a speck of ash from his coat lapel. Satisfied with his appearance, he pushed past the curtain and found himself in an anteroom confronting a pair of sliding oak doors. The solidly built doors were tightly shut, as if guarding the treasure room of some ancient king. *Or his tomb,* the man thought wryly.

He gave the same pattern of knocks as he had used to gain entrance to the building, but this time a voice from within inquired through a tiny wrought-iron grill, "Who comes here?"

"A knight" was his reply.

"A knight of what allegiance?" the voice demanded.

"A knight of the Golden Circle."

"And where are you bound, Sir Knight?"

"From darkness to light, from oppression to freedom; and on to the glorious destruction of all tyrants."

"Enter, Brother Knight."

The room into which the new arrival ventured was grim and unappealing. The windowless walls were bare brick and the air was thick and oppressively dust-laden. He immediately felt as if he were choking.

A single lantern, reeking of rancid whale-oil, sat on a circular table. Around the circle were nine seated men and a single empty chair. No greeting was given as he entered. Instead, the men sat in silence, waiting for the meeting to begin.

At the touch of an unseen doorkeeper, the oak panels slid shut behind him. Directly opposite the entry sat a man whose face was masked. He was sitting rigidly upright in a throne-like chair. Its scroll-carved back rose higher than the others, and the cigar-smoker instinctively looked to its occupant for instruction.

But it was a man with a high forehead and a pointed beard seated on the left who spoke first. "Take your place, Brother Knight" was the order. An imperious wave sent the newcomer to the empty chair.

The bearded man continued, "The first meeting of the Knights of the Golden Circle for the year 1864 will come to order. The situation grows critical, and time is short, so we will dispense with formalities. Each of us has committed to finding and recruiting ten men of uncompromising convictions and unquestioning loyalty to the cause of the South. Each of those ten captains will be responsible for raising a company of soldiers under our command . . . twenty-five hundred men armed and ready to strike . . . within four months."

An outburst of noisy whispers erupted. Biding his time, the speaker grasped his beard thoughtfully, his head inclined toward a young, clean-shaven man seated on his left. The babble around the table concerned the timespan named; no one thought that four months were adequate time to recruit and train such a number for their purpose.

Eventually, the hurried consultations subsided and the speaker resumed his remarks. "There are many good reasons why we must strike soon. Last November, before the victory of that cursed fiend Grant at Chattanooga, we almost had the French and the British convinced to recognize the Confederacy. Gentlemen, we need California, and we need it *now!*"

He paused to allow his words to make their impact, then laid an approving palm on the back of the young man on his left. "We know how to obtain the necessary arms. Will you please tell us Bro . . . , ah, but no. Where are my manners? We should hear first from our new acquaintance. Brother Franklin, late of Washington, D.C."

The man with the cigar crushed it out under his bootheel, stood up and looked at each man seated around the circle, then cleared his throat. He explained how he had been privy to certain war department planning sessions and could speak with authority on Grant's plans for the Union's spring campaigns.

"He will attack Atlanta, that's certain, and Mobile after the fall of Shreveport. It will cut the South in two. We desperately need your aid, brothers. You must prevent the flow of gold and silver from reaching the bloodstained hands of the baboon king, Abe the First. That's why I was despatched here personally: to urge your immediate action and to carry back encouragement to our brave leaders by telling them of your progress."

As Franklin sat down, the leader in the mask nodded his appreciation of this message and spoke at last. "Atlanta and Mobile . . . truly terrifying and calamitous! It must be prevented at all costs. Exactly what our other source has indicated." His voice sounded muffled and sinister.

"What other source?" queried Franklin in consternation. "Only I was sent to bring you this secret and carry back your plans."

"Carry back our plans, eh? No doubt, no doubt. . . . Seize him!"

The two men seated on either side grasped Franklin's arms and pressed them firmly against the table top. A third attacker swung around and dropped a loop of rope over his body, securing it to the chair.

"What is this?" he sputtered. "This is an outrage!"

"Gentlemen," said the bearded man, "I give you not Franklin of the Golden Circle, but Sterling of the Pinkertons!"

The man now identified as Sterling continued to squirm against the rope and protest his innocence. "I am Franklin," he insisted.

"No," corrected the masked leader sternly. "We know that Franklin was killed. Obviously, your masters did not know that we already had gotten word of his death."

Sterling's eyes grew wide with fear, and he tossed and

struggled furiously. "Wait!" he pleaded. "You're mistaken!"

The bearded man slowly shook his head, his pointed whiskers describing a short arc like a swinging dagger-blade. "Goodbye, Mr. Sterling," he said, then lifted a concealed pistol from his lap and shot the helpless Sterling through the heart.

The young, clean-shaven man jumped up in alarm. "Was that necessary?" he demanded. "What if you were wrong? What if this was the real Franklin? How can you be so cold-blooded?"

"Sit down, Brother Hastings," commanded the leader. The burlap sack that served as his mask swelled and shrank ominously as he puffed with anger at the disapproval. "I shall overlook your rash comments this once—only because of your youth and inexperience. But let me warn you: *Never* be critical of a decision of mine ever again, unless you wish to join the Yankee spy. Do you understand?"

Hastings turned ashen. In a stricken voice he muttered, "Of course, General. I forgot my place. Please pardon me." He sat down, tightly grasping his hands together in a vain attempt to stop them from shaking.

"By tomorrow, General, Sterling's body will be a crab's meal at the bottom of the bay," commented the bearded assassin. "And his hotel room is even right now having a mysterious and most destructive fire."

Smiles broke the lingering tension, and the Knights of the Golden Circle seemed genuinely pleased.

"Very good, Brother Perry," commented the masked leader. Ignoring the body slumped across the loop of hemp and the growing dark red stain pooling beneath the chair, he continued, "Now, gentlemen, on to business. Prudence dictates that we conclude these proceedings quickly and reconvene tomorrow night at our alternate location. Remember, from now on, we must be constantly on guard against spies."

CHAPTER 3

The four troopers ranged around the dining table looked awkward and slightly ill at ease. Colonel Mason had ordered them to remain outside because of their trail-worn and mud-spattered condition, but Emily Dawson had overruled him and insisted they come in from the cold.

The cavalrymen were not used to seeing their colonel countermanded, certainly never successfully. They nervously handled the china cups Emily had distributed to them, as if enjoying their coffee would call down the officer's wrath. Each man carried the conviction that dropping a cup could earn him a firing squad.

Deputy Pettibone felt no such reservations. He rattled his cup loudly on its saucer, sloshing the coffee over the sides, then helped himself to a refill and two more cookies from the tray. Colonel Mason frowned at the officious and self-important little man behind the enormous moustache, then continued his conversation with Tom.

"As I was saying, Mr. Dawson, we now believe that the man known as Colonel James was linked to a secret California Confederate society that had a plan—"

"That's right," Pettibone broke in, his whiskers powdered with cookie crumbs. "James was supposed to deliver orders to the men who had been stealing the gold shipments, but he went and got hisself killed by Byrd Guidett sorta accidental-like over a cardgame 'cause Guidett didn't know who he was and—"

"Pettibone," snapped the colonel, "Dawson knows all that! He's the one who rescued the boy from Guidett after the shooting! Now, keep your mouth shut and let me get to the point."

A crestfallen Deputy Pettibone plunged his drooping moustache into his coffee, while the wary troopers exchanged amused glances. "We believe that the outlaw band here on Shadow Ridge was motivated by greed," Mason paused. "Nevertheless, we think the secret society is very real and still active."

"So what's the purpose of your early morning ride?" Tom wondered. "You didn't come all this way to talk about Guidett's gang. What help could I possibly be?" he continued. "I never saw Colonel James before his death."

"Not you," corrected the colonel. "We think that the colored child, Mont, may be able to tell us about others in the group whom James met."

"Colonel," said Emily, her eyes instantly flashing, "Mont is a nine-year-old who still has horrible nightmares from all he's been through. I'll not have him upset needlessly."

Now it was Mason's turn to fidget, picking idly at the crossed-saber insignia on the crown of his hat before replying. "Mrs. Dawson, I know the loss you have personally experienced and I am truly sorry," he said at last.

"But if the Union loses California, the course of the war will be prolonged, at a cost of many thousands of additional lives. What's more to the point for your family is that unless we can stop this conspiracy before it takes root, California may become a battleground as bloody as Shiloh or Gettysburg. If this can be prevented, is it not worth the attempt?"

The round faces of two boys, one pale and one dusky brown, peeked over the rail of their sleeping loft. "Miss Emily, I kin answer questions. It cain't hurt me none."

"All right, Mont," Emily agreed with a sigh. "You boys come on down here."

Colonel Mason attempted to take Mont backward through his memory. "All right," he said kindly, "we already know that you stayed at the home of Thomas Baker down in the valley. While you were there, did you see anyone you had met before, or hear any names mentioned?"

"No suh, I surely didn't," declared Mont.

Trying a different approach, Mason asked, "Well, then, how about before you got to the valley? Did you meet anyone in California that you had seen before in Missouri?"

Mont pondered this question with great intensity, frowning and wrinkling his forehead. Finally he shook his head. "No suh, not so's I recollects."

The colonel was about to give up on this idea, but he tried once more. "Do you remember the names of any other places that you stopped in California?"

Mont gave a wide smile and nodded vigorously. "We was in Frisco! We stopped at a powerful fine hotel too and—" He stopped abruptly as a sudden thought galloped visibly across his face.

Mason looked at Tom and Emily and raised his eyebrows. "What is it, Mont? What did you remember?"

"Well, suh, does you care just about folks I seed in Californy and Missouri?"

The colonel urged Mont to go ahead with whatever he could remember. Pettibone took the opportunity to exhale loudly and crossed his arms over his thin chest, declaring that all this was simply a waste of time.

"In Frisco I did see this man I seed befo', but not in Missouri."

"Where, then, Mont?" urged Emily gently.

"It was the same man what come to see Colonel James in Richmond."

"What?" burst out Colonel Mason. "Richmond, Virginia? Who was this man? What was the meeting about?"

"I don't rightly know, 'ceptin' . . ."

"Yes, go on."

"I heerd them say they was goin' to see Jeff Davis."

"Really!" exclaimed Mason, slapping his knee. "Now we're getting somewhere. Think, Mont, think. What was the man's name?"

Mont shook his head slowly. Even Pettibone sat motionless, waiting for Mont's answer. "I cain't recall no names, but I'd shor nuff know him agin to see him!"

Mason looked extremely pleased.

"Mr. Dawson," Colonel Mason said, "could you bring Mont to Fort Tejon in say, two days' time? I'd like Mont to remember all he can, and then I have something to discuss with you. I also have a prisoner there I want

25

Mont to take a look at."

Avery Hastings stood silently with Jasper Perry on Telegraph Hill, looking down toward the Vallejo Street Wharf and a picturesque scene. Moored at the right of their view was the river steamer *Yosemite*. The side-wheeler's paddle housings reached almost to the level of the wheelhouse, four decks above the waterline. A thin trickle of smoke from the twin stacks showed that the boilers were fired and being kept ready for departure upriver.

But the men's attention was actually directed at two vessels moored one dock closer to their vantage point. One of them was the Pacific mail ship *Arizona*, newly arrived from Panama with letters, parcels and newspapers from "the states." The *Arizona* was a hybrid ship, carrying three masts for sail and a smokestack amidships as well.

The other occupant of the nearer wharf was the United States warship *Cyane*. She had also recently arrived from Panama after a voyage of fifty-one days.

"There is the hen and there the watch dog," said Perry, pointing first toward the mailship and then at the man-of-war.

"What is the turn-of-speed of the *Arizona*?" inquired Hastings.

"Inconsequential, compared to the *Cyane*. The warship is what we must be able to outrun, and then we'll have no difficulty overtaking our quarry."

"Have you a vessel in mind?"

"Come along and I'll show you," replied Perry as he

turned and led the way to a waiting hack.

Montgomery Street was lined with pedestrians and cabs, and they all seemed to be flowing downhill toward the wharf at the end of Jackson Street. Avery raised his eyebrows in question at the seemingly single-minded crowd, but Perry only smiled knowingly and withheld his explanation until the Jackson docks came into view.

Moored there was a schooner bearing the name *Chapman*. It was being unloaded, the swinging cargo nets discharging piles of sacks labelled BEANS onto the dock that was bustling with activity.

"What is so special about this ship?" scoffed Hastings. "A little hundred-ton cargo ship entrusted with freighting beans? You must be joking."

Perry stroked his beard and studied the schooner without comment. A group of onlookers had gathered all around the wharf, and there was a low hum of conversation.

"What is so special about the *Chapman*?" demanded Hastings again. "Why are all these people interested in her?"

"Thirty-eight days from Valparaiso" was Perry's quiet comment.

Hastings was examining the crowd and seemed not to have heard. "That man in the naval uniform is Bissell, commander of the *Cyane*. I believe the man he's speaking with is Ralston of the . . . thirty-eight days from where?"

"Valparaiso," repeated Perry smugly. "If memory serves, it's on the coast of South America."

"But that's—"

"Exactly," Perry interrupted, finally condescending to elaborate. "That is thirteen days faster than it took the *Cyane* to go half as far!"

Suddenly, Hastings' former disdain was replaced with a curious enthusiasm. "And being schooner-rigged, she'll sail closer to the wind and be more maneuverable. She can also be handled by a smaller crew than the square-rigged ships require."

"And there is one more thing in the *Chapman*'s favor," Perry hinted.

"What more could there be? She already outsails one of the fastest warships. This sounds too good to be true."

Jasper Perry's smug look turned into a smirk. "She is for sale. The owners have asked $7500, but I believe we can get her for less."

The air was still and crystal clear as Tom and Mont rode across the toe of the Great Valley toward their meeting with Colonel Mason at Fort Tejon. The peaks they faced stood out in sharp relief, and the furrowed shoulders of the mountains were lightly dusted with powdery snow.

They rode up a treeless, mesquite-covered slope. By turning in his saddle on Duncan's back, Mont could see a hundred miles of the Sierra Nevada mountains sprawled out toward the east and equally as much of the coast range toward the west.

Tom was riding beside him on a young sorrel gelding. With a delighted grin, Mont asked, "Ain't it real plain, Mr. Tom?"

"Isn't what plain, Mont?"

"The smile on God's face when He sees what He done here?"

The two stopped riding to gaze around them in silent admiration. Directly ahead of them was a great cleft in the mountains, which looked as if a giant ax had split the rocks to open a passage.

Tom considered the child's remark and smiled in agreement. Mont's insight had long since ceased to surprise Tom. *The depth of the small boy's understanding must also please the Creator,* Tom thought.

After a few reflective moments, the two urged their mounts forward again, the young red horse dancing sideways at times in his eagerness. Duncan tramped along steadily with the thickly muscled arch of his neck and shoulders leaning into the grade. Duncan had the appearance of a plodding draft animal, but his constantly flicking ears betrayed his alertness.

The wedge-shaped canyon looming ahead had been the subject of old Spanish legends. It was reputed to have been formed when a demon caballero burst out of his underground lair for a diabolical midnight ride.

Tom decided not to share this story with Mont, or the fact that they had recently passed the place where, a few months earlier, Tom and a squad of soldiers had come upon a wrecked stagecoach and another of Byrd Guidett's murder victims. Young Mont was reveling in the grandeur of the scene; why disrupt it with unpleasant reminders of evil and human misery and destruction?

But for Tom himself, it was too late to push back the thoughts and feelings. Forcing its way into his mind was the additional memory that on the day of the stagecoach holdup, his brother Jesse had still been alive.

CHAPTER 4

The dusty brown adobe walls of Fort Tejon's barracks were just barely visible through the screening branches of the leafless cottonwoods and willows along the creek. Once across the rocky ford, the grassy field of the parade ground began and fanned up the hill for three hundred yards.

Tom exchanged greetings with several soldiers he knew from his horse-trading activities. "Hey, Dawson," yelled a stork-thin corporal with a prominent beak to match, "no horses this time?"

Mont received some curious looks. The sight of several whispered conversations told even a nine-year-old mind that his story was being shared with the new recruits.

A pot-bellied man with a bald head and ferocious side whiskers taunted, "What now? Gone to sellin' nig—" His question stopped abruptly with an exhaled gasp as the bony elbow of the corporal slammed into his gut.

"Dawson!" boomed the colonel from the wooden steps of his office. "Thank you for coming. Come in, come in." Turning to his left he said, "Corporal, have Flannery there see to Mr. Dawson's horses."

The two men and the small boy climbed the wooden stairs to Mason's office. "There are more secessionists in this country than the Easterners believe," Colonel Mason remarked to Tom and Mont. The colonel seated himself in a revolving chair next to his roll-top desk. He gestured out the faintly frosted window of his second-story office toward the stretch of valley spreading northward. "Perhaps as many as a third of California's population are from the south or, like yourself, from the border states."

"That doesn't make them secesh," corrected Tom. "Many, like myself, came West to get away from the war."

"True enough," agreed the colonel, "but the outspoken secessionists are not the real problem. The danger lies with those who are outwardly loyal but secretly traitors."

"What do you think this secret society can really accomplish? I keep hearing it claimed they can pull California out of the Union. How, exactly?"

The colonel shook his head. "That's what we need to find out. We know that as lone gunmen or in small bands they are capable of assassination and robbery, but whether they can actually organize an armed insurrection . . ."

Mont was sitting wide-eyed at being included in such a grown-up conversation. Tom gestured toward the boy and asked Colonel Mason, "What do you expect to accomplish by having Mont look at your prisoner?"

"If Mont recognizes him and can tell us where he saw him before, we hope to trace the man's associations in order to get inside the ruling circle of the society. We have some isolated names of those we suspect, but the links between them are missing," replied the colonel.

"Has anything happened to make this more urgent than it was last fall?"

Mason looked at his hands, then up at his saber suspended by a tasselled cord over his desk. With embarrassment in his voice he replied, "Mr. Dawson, I am a soldier, plain and simple. I never wanted to be anything else. But there is . . ." He spoke the next phrase with as much visible distaste as if he had just received a dose of cod liver oil. "There is a *political* issue which cannot be ignored. There is a substantial and growing Northern peace movement. If this spring goes badly for the Union, then Mr. Lincoln's reelection will fail. The new president may sue for peace, even at the cost of letting the seceding states depart."

Tom hunched over in his chair and rubbed his palms together beside a small cast-iron stove. "If that would stop the bloodshed, I'm not so sure it's a bad thing," he commented.

Mason stiffened visibly, but his voice was even and soft when he spoke. "I won't press you with emotional arguments about the sacrifice of those who have already died," he said. "But one fact cannot have escaped your notice: Do you want to see the continued existence of a system that would keep Mont here and millions of others as slaves?"

With the slightest of motions of his hand, Tom beckoned toward the small boy who quietly listened to their conversation. Mont, who had been perched on the edge of the chair, jumped off and ran to stand at Tom's side. "No," Tom said with finality. "No, I do not. Never again."

The fort's jail was housed in a low-roofed adobe building across the frost-browned parade ground. Mason stopped in front of a barred door and indicated it to Mont.

"Take a good look, Mont." The colonel boosted the boy

up to peer through the bars of the guard house. A sullen-faced man with a tan complexion and dark brown hair sat on a rough wooden bench in leg irons even though the cell door was bolted securely.

Tom glanced in while Mont was studying the prisoner. "Shackles inside the cell?" he asked the colonel.

"You of all people know better than to underestimate the ruthlessness of the conspirators. This man killed two of my men before we captured him. Yesterday he clubbed the guard bringing his supper and almost escaped. I'm taking no chances. Seen enough, Mont?"

Mont nodded and Colonel Mason set him down. "Have you seen him anywhere before?"

"No suh, I surely don't think so."

"Think hard," Mason urged. "The man's name is Wilson, or at least that's what he goes by part of the time. Does that help at all?"

Mont asked to be lifted once more, but still shook his head after studying the prisoner a second time. "I never seed him befo'," Mont said. "I'se powerful sorry. They is one thing though . . ."

"Yes, what is it?" urged Mason.

"Well," the boy began, then stopped, looking uncertainly at Tom. "That man in there, he put me in mind of Mistuh Tom."

A few moments later the trio were back in the colonel's office. "Mont's sharp eyes confirmed what I had already noticed," observed Mason. "You bear a remarkable resemblance to our prisoner."

Tom studied the officer warily. "So? What are you driving at?"

"It means, Mr. Dawson, that if you are willing, you may be our method of gaining entrance to the secret society known as the Golden Circle."

"You want me to pretend to be this man Wilson?" asked Tom incredulously. "How do you expect me to carry it off? Isn't he known to the others in the group?"

"No, he isn't. He was imprisoned in the East for activities as a spy. When he escaped, we had word that he would sail for California to join a conspiracy group. Sure enough, we apprehended him when his vessel from Panama put in at Santa Barbara. But no one outside this command knows that, and all the Southern sympathizers have is Wilson's history and general description. That much we coaxed out of him.

"We believe you will be able to infiltrate the Southern sympathizers as well as give Mont an opportunity to keep an eye out for someone he recognizes."

The thump of the iron against the ironing board sounded angry. Tom sat quietly at the kitchen table and waited for Emily to tell him in words what she was indicating every time she clanked the iron onto the hot stove and then tested the temperature of the second iron with the hiss of a drop of water.

"So you're leaving." Her tone was flat when she finally spoke. She set the crease on a flannel shirt sleeve and thumped the hot iron down hard against it.

Tom sipped his coffee and did not reply. Her words were not a question, they were an accusation. She knew that he was leaving her and Nate and Jed for a while. What else could he do?

"For how long?" she asked, not looking up at him.

"I don't right know for sure, Emily, but—"

"What about the ranch? What about . . ." Her voice trailed away. "What about Jed and Nate?" Had she also been wondering what she would do without him?

"This is the best time of year . . . the only time really that I could go. Leave the ranch. Another month there'll be calving to tend to."

"You'll be back in a month, then?" She looked up sharply.

He shrugged his uncertainty. How could he say? "If I'm not . . . well, I already talked to Pastor Swift. He'll lend a hand. And Deputy Pettibone, of course, if there should be any trouble."

"They know what the Union Army has put you up to?"

"Not the details, of course. Not all. Pettibone says not, but Mason believes that what began here with Jesse's dyin' isn't over for us yet. Nobody's fooled about this, Emily. There's still plenty of men out there actively working to push California into the Confederacy." He was trying hard to justify leaving the ranch and the boys . . . and her. She would have none of it.

"And I suppose you're the only one who can put a stop to it?" She raised her chin in a mocking gesture. Occasionally, Tom had seen her look that way at Jesse when there had been a disagreement. Now she challenged him.

"There are hundreds of other men who could go," he replied softly. "But there's only one little Mont to go with them and point out just who a leader of the secesh movement is here in California. The boy *saw him,* Emily, in Richmond! He overheard it all because no one bothered to think that a slave child had the brains to remember all their big talk." He leaned back in his chair and eyed her as she smoothed out the red material of his shirt with a slight touch of gentleness now. "And I don't aim to let anyone else take that poor boy on such a dangerous job. I've kinda grown fond of him, you see?"

She nodded. Her expression was one of misery and some shame that she had not seen it clearly without such a discussion.

"You and your brother . . ." Her voice was laden with emotion. "Before Jesse was . . . before he left . . . we had the same kind of talk. A man has to do what is right. I know that. But, *will* you come back?"

"Of course." He tried to sound light, even though his heart was heavy with the thought of leaving her. And the ranch, of course.

"Jesse *said* he would come back." She put her hand over her mouth and closed her eyes. Tears she thought she had used up squeezed out from between the lids. Jesse had not come back, and Tom alone shared her pain and carried the family responsibilities.

Tom stood and put his hands gently on her shoulders. She did not look at him, for fear of what her eyes might say to him. He kissed her lightly on the forehead—a brotherly kiss, but his voice was thick with emotion. "Emily. Emily. I could walk out the door this morning to mend a fence and if it was my time, well, then, I wouldn't come back. My life and yours are in the hands of the Lord, Emily. I learned that on a long, hard road." He pulled her close against him and she laid her cheek easily against his chest. "So I'll tell you this . . . If it's what the

Lord wants for me, I'll be back in time for the calving. And if it's what the Lord wants for *us,* you'll be here when I return."

CHAPTER 5

The buckboard rattled noisily down the snaking turns of White River Canyon and past the mining town of Tailholt. In some years, crossing the log bridge over White River in January was hazardous because the storm-swollen creek raged through the narrow rocky arroyo. This year the passage was easy and the stream a modest trickle flowing quietly. Despite the early snows in the high country, not much had fallen since, nor had much rain come to the valley. It looked as if last year's drought would continue.

The climb out of the gorge wound around steep-sided buttes of decomposed granite. Dirty white boulders littered the landscape like the discarded toys of a giant's game of marbles.

To help pass the time, Tom told Mont stories from old Indian lore. "See that funnel-shaped rock? The one that looks like an Indian gathering basket? The Yokuts say that it was once an Indian girl who was turned to stone right on that very spot."

"How come?" Mont worried aloud.

"For looking back toward some evil her family was running from. You know, sort of like Lot's wife in the Bible."

"Jest granite, 'stead of salt," Mont observed.

Mont was still looking back at the upside-down cone of

the boulder when the buckboard crested the rise out of the canyon. Spread out before them, yet still a thousand feet lower, lay the great fertile valley—only . . .

"Hey!" Mont exclaimed, spinning around on the spring seat. "Where'd all the valley go? How'd all them clouds get down yonder?"

Tom chuckled, and Duncan's ears flicked back and stayed pointed at the humans as if he too were interested in the explanation. "Tule fog," Tom said. "When it warms up on winter days with no wind, the next night all that marshy land gives off a vapor. It goes on getting thicker and thicker till daybreak, then the sun goes to work burning it off. Sometimes it gets so thick it'll stay like that for weeks till some wind comes to blow it away."

"It look like big, dark water," commented Mont.

Tom agreed. The solid mass of dingy gray fog that stretched across the valley did indeed resemble a stormy sea lapping at the foothills of the Sierras. Here and there a taller knob of rock elevated itself through the mist like an island rising from the waves.

Wispy vines of fog drifted between the branches of the oaks, and soon the rest of the trees were obscured by the floating streamers of mist. A sudden dip in the road plunged the travelers into the dark sea of clammy vapor, and the cheerful yellow sun disappeared. Even the steady clip-clop of Duncan's hooves seemed muffled.

In the dim obscurity, it was easier than ever to conjure up bears out of boulders and lurking Indians from fallen limbs. Mont hoped they would all stay frozen in place until he was past.

Tom also felt oppressed by the grayness. As the fog drew a curtain between them and the ones they loved, his thoughts drifted off into a melancholic study of the trip he and Mont were making, and how long it would pull them away from home.

"Mother, come quick!" Nate's voice rang through the frosty air like the sound an ax makes biting into a cedar tree in the high country. Emily heard the edge of terror in his shout.

Fresh-baked loaves of bread just coming out of the oven spun off toward the corners of the kitchen and the pan dropped unheeded on the floor. Emily grabbed the shotgun from the corner of the front room and raced out the door. What could it be? Her frantic mind conjured up a hundred calamities: a rattlesnake? a mountain lion? the barn was on fire? Jed had hurt himself with the hatchet while chopping kindling?

Nate shouted again from inside the barn, still anxious but more controlled. She was relieved to see Jed sprint around the side of the barn from the woodpile—one less possibility to fret about. Jed warned his mother to be wary in case a wild animal should burst out, but Emily paid no heed and ran headlong into the barn, calling for Nate.

In the same moment that the two charged in, Nate's yell came again, "Mother!" He was inside the box stall of the young red horse. It lay prostrate on the straw, breathing in shuddering gasps. The fine sleek body was seized by a convulsion that started at its neck and rippled down through its whole frame. Every muscle became rigid and taut until it seemed that the flesh would tear apart the overstretched skin. Even the horse's lips curled back from his teeth in a horrid parody of a grin.

Just as suddenly, the grip of the seizure relaxed. The gelding was instantly gasping for breath as if he had been held under water and almost drowned. He began to thrash his limbs in all directions, frantically pawing and snorting. He threw his head backward and forward, trying to escape the grasp of pain that had clutched his whole body. It was too great to be borne.

"Nathan!" Emily screamed. "Get out of there!"

Before Nate could make a move, he was bowled over by a fling of the sorrel's head. Thrown against the partition of the stall, he landed with a thud that left him dazed in the dirt. "Get up!" his mother cried. Jed vaulted the boards of the stall and scooped up his little brother like a sack of potatoes.

By the time Jed boosted Nate over the stall into his mother's waiting arms, he was able to speak again and pleaded, "Help him! Help him!"

"He's colicked," said Emily firmly. "I'll do what I can, but . . ." At the mute entreaty in Nate's eyes, she stopped and left the sentence unfinished. "Are you all right, Nate? Able to help?"

Stifling a great shuddering sob, Nate controlled himself and pulled himself erect. "Yes, Mother," he agreed. "What can I do?"

"Run into the house and bring me the jug of molasses. Get an unopened crock of sausage out of the pantry. Pour the teakettle into the bucket and fill the bucket with cool water, then bring everything out to me. Quick as you can, now."

Before the final instructions had even left her mouth, the boy was out of the barn and dashing toward the house. She called after him, "Mind the kettle! Don't burn yourself." To Jed she said, "All right, Jed, we've got to try to get him up. Quickly now, before another seizure takes him."

Even as she spoke the horse became rigid once more. In the extremity of the convulsion, he ceased to breathe and his eyes took on a fixed, glassy stare. The color of his exposed gums turned a deadly white. "We're losing him," Emily shouted, and just as unmindful of her own safety as she had been worried about Nate's, she rushed into the pen. She threw her weight on the sorrel's rib cage, forcing him to breathe.

After a few seconds that seemed like an eternity, the horse came out of the spasm. This time he was so weak that he could not even swing his head, let alone thrash his legs.

"Help me roll him upright," Emily said to Jed. It took all their combined strength just to move the horse off his side and onto his stomach. "Grab those feed sacks," she ordered, "and stuff them along here next to the wall. We have to keep him from getting down flat again."

By this time Nathan had returned with a double-arm load of the things Emily had requested. Tears were streaming down his cheeks, but he was all business when he set the water bucket down and lined up the molasses and the sausage crock for his mother's inspection. "Now what?" he asked manfully.

"Now pray," she instructed. Into the warm water she

poured a half-gallon of cottonseed oil that had been covering the sausages as a preservative. To this she added a pint of molasses. "Get the funnel with the longest spout you can find," she told Jed.

When he had returned, Emily had Jed pull the horse's tongue out the side of his mouth and hold it there. With his other hand he directed the spout of the funnel down the animal's throat. "Pray hard," Emily said again to both the boys. "If he seizes while we're pouring this down him, he'll strangle for sure."

"Wait!" demanded Nate. With his eyes screwed tight shut, he made a fervent request with moving but soundless lips. "All right," he said at last. "Do it now."

Emily poured the funnel full, then massaged the gelding's neck until swallowing motions appeared and the liquid in the funnel went down. She paused to look for signs of another convulsion, and when none appeared, began to pour again. This process was repeated and repeated until every drop of two gallons of fluid had been drained into the animal.

"Now," Emily said, "let's see if we can get him up." The warm mixture and all the human attention seemed to ease the horse's panic. He appeared to understand what was wanted even if he could not oblige. "Rock him," she said, and the boys sprang to obey.

After several heaves and shoves and coaxing pulls on his mane, the red horse rose unsteadily to his feet. Emily put the loop of a lead rope loosely around his neck, and motioned for Jed to open the stall gate. Twenty paces down to the end of the barn, a short pivot, and twenty paces back. "Keep him moving," she instructed Jed, who took over from her after ten turns around the barn. "We'll need to do this turnabout all day and through the night, till whatever bad he got into works its way out. I'll go heat more water so we can dose him again in a bit. Mind," she said looking at Nate intently, "if he goes to take another fit, keep clear of him."

"Yes'm," agreed Nate. "We'll walk him good. Won't we, Jed?" The two brothers started off on the first of hundreds of little circuits inside the barn.

Emily looked out the window toward the barn for the tenth time in an hour. She watched the flickering lantern light shining through the half-open door until the shadows of boys and horse passed, then she returned to her sewing.

At least she tried to concentrate on the never-ending pile of mending. Even when not fretting about the boys, she was worrying about Tom and Mont. She wished now that she had objected more to their going. She thought about how difficult life on the ranch was even when they were here. There were always problems with the stock, or some machinery broken down, or something on the house, barn or corrals that needed to be fixed. She sighed. Why compound all those things by going hundreds of miles away on business that properly belonged to the Union army?

The truth was, she and her little brood had grown very comfortable, despite the constant stresses of ranch life, and she hated to see that comfort disturbed. Having Tom around made her feel secure, almost like having her husband again.

She stopped and shook her head. That direction of thinking was no good at all. Best to not dwell on it.

Emily roused herself to look at the time: past midnight already. She decided to go out and check on the boys, even though their turn was not up for another hour.

At the stable she found a weary and leaden-eyed Jed tramping in smaller and smaller circles, leading a droopy looking red horse. At first she could not see Nathan at all, then spotted him, curled up like a cat, asleep on the feed sacks.

"Jed, I'll take over now. You get your brother and go on in and get some sleep. I'll come for you when I need you."

"Huh?" was all the reply he could manage.

Shaking the slumbering Nate, and putting his hand in Jed's, she led them to the door and pointed them toward the house. Then she resumed the circuits of the barn.

The air inside the barn was growing colder until it penetrated the coat Emily was wearing. She paused in her pacing to look around for something to throw over her shoulders. Her eyes lit on the empty feed sack Nathan had been curled up with, and she shook it out.

A scrap of paper fluttered free. Emily wondered if it had fallen out of Nate's jacket. She retrieved it, and carried it till the next pass under the lantern gave her light enough to read.

In scrawled pencil marks the unsigned note read: DAWSON—THIS COULD HAPEN TO ALL YER STOCK. KEEP CLEER OF ARE BIZNES.

CHAPTER 6

Visalia was the county seat of Tulare County in the Great Valley of California and was two days' travel down from Shadow Ridge. It stood on a plain noted by the old Spanish explorers for its grove of magnificent oaks. The confluence of the rivers draining the Sierras made the location a natural way point for hunters and prospectors as well as those who would sell to them and buy from them.

It was also home to a large population of people whose sympathies clearly lay with the Confederacy. The local newspaper, the *Equal Rights Expositor*, had an outspoken editor who saw every issue as an opportunity to brand the Union army as invaders, Lincoln as a tyrant, and Yankees as fools, generally. He was something of a local hero but had earned himself some enemies as well.

The paper's third issue of 1864 was especially strong. Half the columns were devoted to editorials deploring the brutality of Northern aggression. Garrison, the editor, took particular aim at the establishment of Camp Babbitt, near Visalia.

The ranchers and farmers in the valley had always been nervous about Indian raids sweeping in from the eastern reaches of the Sierras. When the regular army forces had been withdrawn from the valley to carry out patrol assignments in the deserts of the Southwest, the ranchers' concern increased even further. A volunteer force had been raised to fill in for the reassigned regulars. Camp Babbitt was the headquarters for a portion of the Second

Cavalry, California Volunteers.

Lieutenant Colonel William Hardy commanded the detachment of horse soldiers at Babbitt. He and his patrol had just returned from two weeks in the high lonesome, chasing Indians who seemed little more substantial than the rapidly melting snowflakes.

Sparse snow had not meant sparse cold, however. Hardy and his troopers had gone to bed with icy winds howling through the passes and into their tent flaps. They had been treated to the experience of watching their breath solidify into ice crystals inside their tents. There had been no escaping the bone-chilling cold.

As if this were not bad luck enough, Hardy had received the additional indignity of coming down with the worst fever of his life. It was fortunate it came near the end of the ride. Now he was huddled in the eight-by-eight cabin that served him as both quarters and office. A shawl was drawn around his shoulders, and his feet soaked in a pan of steaming water to which half a bottle of turpentine had been added.

There was a timid knock at his door. "What is it?" he croaked angrily.

The door opened a fraction and a wisp of fog drifted in, followed by a cautious Corporal Brant. "Sorry to disturb you, sir," the corporal began.

"Get on with it!" exploded the colonel. The last word was punctuated by a particularly violent sneeze.

"Yes, sir, sorry, sir. The Visalia telegrapher reports the line is down, sir."

"Indeed? And since when is that army business? Tell him to attend to it himself. That's what he . . . he . . . *achoo!*"

The corporal waited patiently until Hardy finished sneezing and concluded his sentence, ". . . what he gets paid for!"

"Yes, sir. But he found that the line had been cut, sir. In twelve places, sir."

"What!?" Hardy demanded, standing upright and almost tripping over the pan. "Blasted secesh!" The colonel swore, sneezed again and bit his tongue, which made him swear even louder. "Get Captain Warner. Tell him to take . . . what now, Corporal?"

Corporal Brant backed up a step before replying, which put his shoulders squarely against the cabin door. "Captain Warner is not in camp, sir. You sent him and Lieutenant Miller to Fort Tejon."

Hardy angrily dismissed the rest of the explanation with an irritated gesture. "I remember, Corporal. All right, sound assembly. Company A ready in fifteen minutes. That will be all, Corporal."

Brant fumbled with the door to make his exit. By the time he got it open, another monstrous sneeze and another violent burst of profanity propelled him out into the fog.

A handbill nailed to the trunk of a large oak caught Mont's attention. "What do it say?" he asked.

"Go on, you can make it out," Tom urged.

"Tonight," the child read, "Perfesser William Brewer will speech—"

"Speak," Tom corrected.

"Speak on the . . . what did the rest say?" Mont asked since the buggy had by this time rolled past the announcement.

"It says that Brewer will speak on the drought in California." Tom added, "I've heard of Brewer. He's part of a group making a survey . . . you know, maps and such . . . of California's mountains."

"Kin we go?"

"I don't see why not. We're staying the night in Visalia, and we can find a place to camp close by the lecture hall."

Across the street from the newspaper office of the *Equal Rights Expositor* was the Oddfellows Hall. The hall was a two-story affair with whitewashed board-and-bat siding. Downstairs it contained two small offices, one for a doctor and the other for an attorney. Only the physician's space was occupied for the time being; the lawyer had gotten himself killed in a stage holdup only a week earlier.

The lodge room upstairs was often used for community gatherings, town meetings, and the like, as well as serving as the temporary home of the Cumberland Presbyterian Church. The single large room that filled the second floor had a raised platform at the end opposite the door. The backless wooden benches could seat close to a hundred if closely packed, and half-a-hundred more could be accommodated with standing room.

There were nowhere near that number present for William Brewer's lecture. When Tom and Mont climbed the outside wooden stairs that led to a balcony outside the meeting hall, only thirty or so had come out on the foggy night to listen to the professor of agricultural chemistry.

The tall man with the stooped shoulders was already speaking: "And just how severe is the present drought? The year 1862 produced over twenty-four inches of rain in San Francisco, while in 1863 the same area received only three inches. What is worse, no rainstorm of any consequence has struck the southern half of the state since last January—twelve months ago."

Standing in the doorway listening was a short, skinny man with a disorderly ring of white hair around his otherwise bald knob of a head. In between nodding at what Brewer was saying, the small man cast an occasional look over his shoulder at the newspaper office. He gave no evidence of intending to step aside from blocking the entrance to the room, but continued to brace himself between the doorposts like a miniature Samson in training for the destruction of the Oddfellows temple.

Tom cleared his throat by way of asking for permission to pass, and the short figure did in fact whirl around at the sound. But instead of moving out of the way, he stretched out a bony finger down toward the street and broke into a cackle of laughter that Mont thought would have done credit to the black speckled hen at the Dawson farm.

Turning to see what the source of amusement was, they spotted a bedraggled troop of horsemen riding wearily into town. The men's heads drooped, and so did the heads of their mounts.

"Who are they?" Tom questioned cautiously.

The man stopped in the middle of his cackling and turned to stare at Tom. "Who are *you* is the question." But before waiting for an answer, he swung back to the scene below and said, "Them's farmers playin' at being

49

soldiers," and went into another gale of raucous laughter.

"What's the matter, toy soldiers?" he shouted down at them. "Can't find no Injuns to play with? Can't find no Rebs neither? Best you go back to your plows, boys, if you can still find them!" He laughed uproariously at his own jokes, and everyone at Brewer's lecture turned around to view the commotion.

A trooper muttered something and another nodded tersely. A third made a little louder grumble and stopped his horse's shambling walk.

Usually Colonel Hardy was a stickler for discipline and would not have tolerated speaking in ranks, but he was feeling too rotten to care. Besides, the little man's comments stung.

The self-appointed tormentor spoke again. "It's no wonder the blue dogs of the Baboon King are gettin' whipped. They can't any of 'em fight any better than you!"

Hardy's Troop A from Camp Babbitt had covered thirty miles out and back. They had repaired a dozen places where the telegraph line had been cut. But when they came to a thirteenth break, they found that it was not repairable. It was not just cut, the line itself was nowhere in sight. For the space of four telegraph poles, the wire had been stripped completely and carried away.

Colonel Hardy had been alternately sneezing and coughing as the unit rode back into town. The vandals had left plenty of tracks to follow—tracks that ended beside Pronghorn Slough where the last telegraph pole perched next to a stagnant sheet of green, slimy ooze. But the slough ran for miles in both directions, giving the rebels plenty of maneuvering room to hide their trail.

Something in Hardy snapped. The fever and chills, the agonizing ride and the salty remarks rubbed into open wounds had pushed him over the edge. In a voice that sounded like a coffee grinder he ordered, "Seize that secesh and his treasonous paper!"

It was then that Tom realized the little man was Garrison, the infamous editor of the secesh newspaper. Not to be deterred, the head man of the *Equal Rights Expositor* rushed down the stairs toward his business shouting, "Ned! Seth! Get the guns!"

Six troopers moved to carry out Hardy's order to seize the paper, and Corporal Brant went after Garrison. The banty rooster of a man lowered his shoulder and plunged straight into the surprised corporal, bowling him completely over. But two more soldiers had greater success, tackling Garrison and tying him up.

The two employees of the *Expositor* looked up from their printing duties to see half-a-dozen soldiers burst into the one-room building. Seth, the printer's devil, threw himself toward a cupboard beside the press and flung it open.

The one named Ned rushed toward the counter across the front of the room, reaching it just as a trooper named Stillwell vaulted over it. Ned's sweeping right fist caught Stillwell on the point of chin at the exact moment that the man's toes touched the floor. The impact lifted him so forcefully that it appeared he jumped backward up onto the counter like a puppet suddenly jerked upward on its strings.

Brandishing a pistol, Seth spun from the cupboard, but

a soldier on each side of him caught his arms at the same moment. There was a resounding roar as the Remington forty-four exploded, but the shot went into the ceiling.

Ned turned from cold-cocking Stillwell to help his friend, but two more troopers jumped him from behind and wrestled him to the ground. The three men rolled over and over, crashing into the compositing bench. Slugs of type rattled and bounced, flying through the air like spent bullets.

Jerking free of his attackers, Ned grabbed up the plate of text he had been completing. He swung it sideways into a soldier's face, smashing the man backward into a wall and leaving the word TYRANNY neatly incised across his cheekbone. An instant later, the butt of a carbine struck Ned behind the ear and he collapsed in a heap.

Two more cavalrymen ran into the *Expositor* office carrying a long coil of rope. As Tom and Mont watched from their balcony perch across the street, the end of the rope was soon brought back outside and made fast to Corporal Brant's saddlehorn, while the bound Garrison screeched a protest.

At a nod from Hardy, Brant applied the spurs to his bay, which responded with a sudden spurt forward. There was a thunderous crash, and Garrison's printing press erupted through the wood of the counter and tore apart the doorway and one porch support before landing in the road.

Garrison raged and cursed, savaging all within sight and sound with a blistering string of foul oaths. The porch roof of the newspaper office tilted crazily and an ominous screeching suggested that the entire building might collapse.

As Tom looked on with mounting horror, Brant returned, fashioning a noose in the rope he had retrieved. The corporal looked expectantly toward Hardy, who gave a grim nod, then Brant tossed the coil over a nearby oak limb and tied it off so that the loop dangled eight feet off the ground.

Another trooper brought his horse alongside Garrison, who was roughly boosted into the saddle. The spindly editor was led toward the waiting noose.

"No!" shouted Tom, almost involuntarily. "Don't!" To Mont he said, "Stay up here. Whatever happens, stay up here!"

Tom vaulted over the railing, landing cat-like on his feet. He ran full force into the man holding the horse. The violence of the impact rolled the man completely over backward. The horse spooked and reared, tumbling Garrison off on the ground.

Grabbing the young rancher from behind, Brant roughly pinned Tom's arms to his sides. The man Tom had knocked down rose and drew back his fist, aiming a blow at Tom's chin.

Tom twisted Brant sideways, and the hapless corporal caught the blow intended for Tom on his right ear. Howling in pain, Brant released his hold, and Tom added an elbow smash to Brant's face.

Snatching up his fallen rifle, the other soldier levelled a two-foot-long bayonet at Tom's throat. Stopping perfectly still, but without flinching, Tom called out loudly, "Colonel! Don't do this! Enough!"

Colonel Hardy turned his flushed face toward Tom. The officer's red-rimmed eyes had difficulty focusing on the man who stood before him. Hardy's breath was ragged and a shiver worked its way down his spine and out to the ends of his fingers. He looked the part of a madman.

"Colonel," Tom repeated, "don't do this. Think what you are doing. Think of the women and children." Tom slowly gestured toward the crowd of people huddled on the balcony of the Lodge Hall where all thought of Brewer's talk on the drought was forgotten.

Hardy turned his feverish gaze upward to take in the onlookers, then at the oak where the noose was dangling. Despite the chill, beads of sweat broke out on the colonel's forehead and ran down into his eyes. He brought a gloved hand up to clear them. When he took it down again, new clarity had replaced the glazed stare of a moment before. He looked at Tom and the group of soldiers preparing to lynch the editor, as if seeing them for the first time. "You there! You men, stop that! Hold that horse, Brant!"

There was grumbling from some of the cavalrymen, but most moved sheepishly to comply, glad that some force had stopped them short of the hanging. "Brant," Hardy croaked at the corporal, "the others are to be released. Mr. Garrison is under arrest. Bring him along."

With no word of acknowledgement to Tom or the others viewing the scene, Troop A gathered themselves and moved off toward Camp Babbitt. Ned and Seth were left to nurse their wounds and collect ink bottles and overturned chairs.

Ned walked unsteadily outside, ducking to pass under the sagging porch roof. He rubbed a huge lump behind his ear and groaned. Stumbling toward Tom, he extended his hand. "Thanks, mister. I figured old Garrison for a goner, and maybe me an' Seth for after. If there's anything you ever need . . . what's your name, anyways?"

Tom looked down at a tug on his coat sleeve to find Mont trying to get his attention about something. . . . "It's Wilson," Tom said. "My name is Wilson."

"Are you just passing through, Mr. Wilson?"

"We're on our way to Frisco. I've been told we'll find friends there who think like Garrison."

"Frisco." Ned rubbed his aching head thoughtfully, as if making a careful assessment before saying any more. "Well, Mr. Wilson, I can steer you to a mighty good place to stay. Look for the Tehama House Hotel. You'll find the company to your liking there. And before you leave, let me send a message with you. You just give it to the person at the desk. He'll take care of the rest."

CHAPTER 7

The threatening note fluttered in the hand of Deputy Pettibone. He squinted at the words and then looked at the weary sorrel gelding still being led slowly around the barn by Jed in the morning light.

"You're mighty lucky you ain't callin' a crew to haul a dead horse out of that barn this mornin'. How'd you save him?" he asked Emily.

"I didn't think of poison. It looked like a bad case of colic, so first thing we did was pray; then we dosed him with cottonseed oil and . . . well, we've been walking him all night."

"And you all by yourself, too. A woman alone faced with such a thing." He clucked his tongue sympathetically. "That brother-in-law of yours done run off already, has he?"

"Not run off." Emily did not like his tone, even though there had been times through the ordeal when she, herself, had angry thoughts toward Tom. "But he and Mont are gone on their business."

"Well, now," Deputy Pettibone suddenly seemed real interested. He looked at the note again. "Well, well. And you and these here boys saved the horse. And what about the rest of your stock, Widow Dawson? Says right here . . ."

Emily put a hand to her aching forehead. How could she keep an eye on every animal on the ranch? How could she prevent anyone from carrying out a threat to poison the Dawson livestock? And whom could she trust?

"Tom said you would help if we had any trouble."

"Don't know how even the Union Army could stand guard against something like this." He folded the note and slipped it into his coat pocket. "Where's Tom headed?"

She paused before answering. Hadn't Tom told even Pettibone where he was going? "San Francisco."

"Well, then. Well, well, Widow Dawson. I'll tell you what I can do for you. I'm headed up to Fort Tejon, and then on to Los Angeles myself. I'll stop at the fort and inform the captain what's happened here. Tell 'im he oughtta get word to that brother-in-law of yours. In the meantime, since the Union has borrowed your man, they oughtta send a few blue-bellies this-away to help you out, I figger."

Emily nodded with relief. How grateful she was that Pettibone had stopped to check on her and the boys this morning. If Tom had not talked to the deputy, she felt it could be no accident that he had arrived just in the hour of her greatest desperation. "Will you stop and ask Parson Swift to come out before you leave, Deputy? I'm in need of comforting after last night. I surely am."

"We must have a suitable captain," demanded Jasper Perry. "An experienced man, someone who knows these waters . . . a man with sand, who will stop at nothing."

Hastings looked crestfallen. "Is my appointment to mean nothing, then? My commission in the Confederate States Navy names me as captain."

Hastily hiding a mocking smile behind his hand, Perry said soothingly, "Avery, I mean no offense! You will have the command of the vessel, of course. But you agree to the wisdom of having a sailing master, do you not?"

Avery gave in to the soundness of this suggestion. "Do you have someone in mind?"

"By the stroke of good fortune, I do!" Perry explained that the man he intended to recruit for the conspiracy had once been an officer on the Pacific mail steamship *Oregon*. "He knows the routes of the mail ships and the thinking of their owners and officers. Come on, I think I know where to find him."

Perry led Hastings toward a shabby waterfront saloon.

The name stenciled on the filthy smoked glass window had been "Devil May Care," but when one pane had been broken in a brawl, half the sign was destroyed and never replaced. What remained in a quarter arc of dingy suggestiveness read "Devil May."

Inside the dimly lit saloon were a handful of customers drinking toasts to midmorning forgetfulness. As Avery stood in the doorway, he saw a wrinkled crone leap back from riffling a rummy's pockets as he lay sleeping across a table. When the hag saw that neither newcomer was the law, she brazenly returned to exploring the man's coat.

A nudge in Hastings' ribs startled him out of his disgusted stare. "Keep one hand on your watch and the other on your wallet," Perry hissed, but he was smiling as he said it. Jasper Perry did not seem out of his element at all.

At a corner table that could barely be seen in the artificial gloom sat a lone man with a squat body and a dark, leathery face. His broad features included a nose that was little more than a shapeless lump of red-veined gristle. Sagging jowls mirrored the corners of his downturned mouth.

The man was dressed in the dark blue denim of a sailor, so his form faded into the black shadowy recess. His face and one bandaged hand seemed to float above the greasy table like apparitions in a spiritualist's show.

Perry approached the figure without hesitation, although Hastings hung back a pace. "Captain Law?" Perry asked tentatively.

For a long moment there was no reply. Avery wondered if they had made a mistake, or if perhaps the man was deaf, or in a drunken stupor. Perry was on the point of repeating himself when the sailor held up his bandaged left hand.

"I am not captain no more, they say. I am a cripple and cannot command, they say. The infernal deep take them all, I say! I have more to captain with in these stumps than they in all their whole worthless carcasses!"

"How did it happen?" Avery burst out. He was instantly sorry that he had spoken, for Captain Law's upturned eyes engaged his in a murderous stare. The pale blue, watery orbs bulged slightly from their sockets and reminded Hastings of the staring eyes of a drowned man he had once seen fished out of a river. *Dead lights,* he thought.

"Was a thieving kanaka, what done it. Caught him at the ship's stores. Would not take his medicine like a man. Fought me, he did. Me! His lawful captain!"

"You lost your fingers protecting ship's property and then the ungrateful owners discharged you?" said Perry in a voice surprisingly full of sympathetic indignation.

"Claimed I need not have killed him, they did," continued Law. He leaned back from the table to display a sheath knife with a folding marlin-spike in its handle. "Had a right tussle, too."

"Of course," blurted Avery. "He cut off your fingers in the fight—surely the owners can see that it was self-defense."

"Not so, neither," corrected Law. " 'Twas not in the fight I lost 'em. When I went to put the noose around his scrawny neck to haul him to the maintop he bit one of 'em clean off, but the rest the doctor chopped. Gangrene from the stinkin' dog."

Perry looked at Hastings significantly, then said to Law, "Captain, we have a business proposition to discuss with you."

Avery Hastings hoped that he did not look as green as he felt.

The Market Street scene unrolling in front of Mont's view overwhelmed his nine years' worth of experience in a way he had never felt before. San Francisco was so amazing that despite this being his second visit, he was goggle-eyed. Three-and-four and even five-story buildings loomed all around, and hundreds of curious people walked or rode into his attention.

A covey of Chinamen in quilted cotton pajama-suits shuffled by, chattering to one another in singsong cadence. Their pigtails and round cloth caps were bobbing in time, and they were oblivious to Mont's stare.

From the other direction, three men in suits and bowler hats were riding two-wheeled contraptions with pedals on the front axles. Tom said that the machines were called velocipedes. Mont wanted to know if they were somehow related to the many-legged critters he had seen up in the mountains.

A horse-drawn streetcar made its appearance, announced by the plodding clop of hooves and the musical ringing of the bells for fares and crossings. Pursuing the streetcar were two nondescript mutts of indifferent breeding. The dogs were not actually running after the vehicle, but kept a steady trot close behind. At the corner stop closest to where Tom and Mont were standing, an impressive figure in military garb stepped from the coach. In his epauletted uniform and plumed top hat, he plunged through the crowd directly toward them, followed closely by the two dogs.

Several passersby tipped their hats to the portly, bearded man with the brass-headed cane and his canine attendants. Mont overheard him addressed as "Your Excellency," "Your Honor," "Your Highness," and even "Your Magnificence."

With single-minded purpose in his step, this high potentate, whoever he was, walked straight over to the two of them as if their meeting were prearranged. Stopping right in front of Tom, the man rapped the tip of his cane on the ground three times, as if calling a courtroom to attention.

"We note from your apparel that you are from the interior reaches of our domain," said the individual in the gold-braided dress coat. "We would inquire as to the state of our affairs in the hinterlands."

Mont wondered who the "we" was—decided that it must mean the dogs who were now seated politely one pace behind.

If Mont was confused about the plural form of address, Tom was just as baffled by the questions. "Well, I—" he began, then stopped.

"Come, come, man, speak up. Is aught amiss with your home province? Is our attendance required to redress error and quell rebellion?"

Fortunately, Tom was spared further interrogation by the aid of a helpful newsboy who had been listening to the exchange with amusement. "Scuse me, Emperor, your Highness. Jim Daly at your service. These here vis'ters don't speak any English. They are just arrived from . . ." Here the boy pivoted quickly to slip Tom a broad wink, "from Egypt."

"Splendid!" exclaimed the emperor, his ostrich plume waving with delight. "Welcome to our country! Quick, lad," he said to the newsboy, "proclaim us properly, Master Daly."

"Yes, sir, your Majesty. This here is Emperor Norton the First of America."

"And?" prompted the emperor.

"Oh, I almost fergot. Protector of Mexico."

"Quite right. Well done. Well, we must be off. We are late for luncheon with the cabinet. Matters of state. Master Daly, direct the ambassador to come round and present his credentials when he has the proper formal attire, and render him every assistance." He snapped the ferrule of his cane alongside his hat in a kingly gesture.

"Bow," hissed Jim. "Bow, 'fore he gets mad." Tom and Mont obediently bent their necks.

Emperor Norton smiled pleasantly and clicked his fingers. "Come Bummer. Come Lazarus. To luncheon." The emperor continued his stately progress down Market Street, accompanied by his bulldog and terrier comrades. Tom, Mont, and the newsboy watched him until he paused before a sign that read: Golden Nuggett Saloon—Free Lunch. Emperor Norton pivoted with military precision and entered the saloon at the head of his happily wagging cabinet officers.

"Who was that?" burst out Tom with a suddenly exhaled breath and laugh.

Jim grinned. "Emperor Norton? He's just a poor crazy

man what lost a fortune—and then lost his mind. Thinks he's royalty."

"Why isn't he locked up?"

Shocked and angry, the newsboy shot back, "He don't hurt nothin'. Everybody here is a little crazy . . . him a mite more'n most . . . but we like him thataway!"

"No offense, son," soothed Tom. "Thanks for explaining. Maybe you can help us with something else. We just left off our rig at the livery stable here, and now we need to get to the Tehama House."

"Tehama? Sure enough. Corner of California and Sansome." Jim proceeded to give directions, concluding with which stop to leave the streetcar. "You can see it from there," he said.

"Much obliged," said Tom, reaching in his pocket.

"Naw," said the newsboy, looking down the street toward the Golden Nuggett. "Wouldn't be right. It was a—what ya say, royal command."

"Then consider this a token presented by the ambassador of Egypt," Tom laughed and handed over a dime.

"Leave off tellin' me how sure of success you be, and splice me the cable of your plan instead," demanded Captain Law. The room on the third floor of the Tehama Hotel was occupied by Law, Perry, and Avery Hastings.

"Do you swear to be true to—" Hastings began.

"You can leave off unfurling any of your oaths, too," snorted Law. "I give you my word to say naught of your scheme. . . . That will have to serve, for I'll not promise more without the full chart of the voyage." His pale blue eyes flashed in defiance that clearly read: "You need me more than I need you."

Perry and Hastings withdrew to a corner of the room for a hasty consultation. Law meanwhile wandered over to the window looking out on Sansome Street. He studied the forms of several passing women, squinting first one eye and then the other against the glare of the sun. His attention briefly touched on a tall, well built man who walked up Sansome with a small black child at his side. Hastings called Law back to the table.

"All right, Captain," said Avery reluctantly. "We will trust you with our entire plan, and then you can make up your mind."

Inclining his bulldog face in approval, and carefully laying his injured left hand on the tabletop, Law prepared to listen.

"We intend to purchase the *Chapman* and outfit her with enough arms and men to seize a Pacific mail steamship," Avery explained.

"Hold fast there a minute," objected Law. "And what of the *Cyane*? You might stop one mail ship, but they'll have an escort after that. Your puny schooner may outrun 'em, but it can't outfight a warship."

Jasper Perry took over the narration, his brooding eyes growing more animated with his enthusiastic portrayal of the conspiracy. "We mean to use the steamer to transport men to seize the arsenal at Benecia and the warships at Mare Island. Next, we'll sail down and capture or destroy the *Cyane* and occupy Fort Point."

"Lay off the point instead," remarked Law, shaking his head. "Where will this army come from?"

"We have trusted lieutenants who are even now

recruiting loyal sons of the South from the gold fields between here and the Comstock. When the time comes, they'll be ready. But we must do our work as well, to be able to furnish transport to the attack on Benecia and what follows."

Law appeared to be considering this proposition. He stared hard at the stumps of his damaged hand, maybe contemplating the fingers that were no longer there. Hastings felt uneasy around the sea captain and wished that they could hurry and conclude their business. He was glad that he was leaving for the Comstock and would not have to deal with Law.

At last Law said, "And you want me to be master aboard *Chapman*, is that it? To command a pirate ship on a pirate's mission?"

"Privateer," Avery protested. "Duly authorized—"

"Bah!" Law snorted again, like the sound of a signal cannon firing. "Does a man's neck stretch any less if he be called 'privateer,' when those that catches him decides to hang him? And you?" he added, sneering into Avery's face. "Mind you, it's all one to me. There's some as would say that pirate is a step up from the days when I was captain aboard a slaver on the New Orleans run. . . . All right, here stand my terms: *Chapman* is mine when the job is done and . . ." He paused to wave his bandaged hand under Avery's nose. "I want one thousand dollars, gold, afore we start. Do you have it?"

Hastings and Perry exchanged looks and decided to tell Law the truth. "No," Avery reported. "We only had enough for earnest money for the *Chapman*. We don't yet have the funds to complete the purchase or outfit her, or pay you what you ask."

"And what will you do about it?"

"That is not your concern," retorted Perry. "We will have the additional amount soon. In fact, we want you to make out a list of equipment needed aboard the *Chapman*, and we will order it for delivery in two weeks. Our agent will have secured the money by then."

CHAPTER 8

With its green steep gabled roof and white clapboard siding, Mount Carmel Presbyterian Church was a jewel among the surrounding buildings of Greenville in the valley below Shadow Ridge. The bell in its steeple had rung out to announce the election of Lincoln, and some months later, the beginning of the war between North and South. For a time, discussion of politics had been off-limits within its sanctuary. But the death of Emily Dawson's husband by the treachery of a member of the congregation had split the church. It had caused Emily herself to support the Northern cause with renewed dedication.

This morning several pews were empty as the congregation rose to sing the *Battle Hymn of the Republic*. Even empty pews did not dim the fervor of those who sang and then prayed for the restoration of the Union. Those who supported the Southern cause met in a newly framed plainer building just across the street. Their voices bellowed the tune of *Onward Christian Soldiers* in an attempt to drown out their Yankee neighbors. In Greenville, only the dusty road separated North and

South, but the gulf between neighbors and onetime friends was as wide as an ocean.

Pastor Swift preached a mighty sermon from the thirty-seventh Psalm. *"Fret not thyself because of evildoers. . . ."* He pounded the plain wooden pulpit and his gray-streaked beard trembled with righteous indignation as he gestured out the window toward the congregation that had seceded from the union of his church.

"For evil men will be cut off," he shouted, striking the pulpit again with energy that would have rivaled old John Knox himself! "A little while, and the wicked will be no more!" He waved his arm toward the Southern Baptist building. "Though you look for them, they will not be found!"

Nate grimaced at these words. Jed rubbed his cheek thoughtfully. Both boys had told their mother they would rather have their old school friends back in the pews with them instead of having swords pierce their hearts as Pastor Swift said. The majority of their classmates cheered the victories of Jefferson Davis and openly cursed Lincoln's army. Would they ever be friends again?

Emily squeezed the hands of her sons when they leaned forward to whisper such thoughts to each other. Even a church, it seemed, was not the proper place to preach political peace and reconciliation.

"The Lord loves the just and will not forsake His faithful ones," Pastor Swift preached on. "They will be protected forever, but the offspring of the wicked will be cut off."

So much for the children of Southern sympathizers. Well, if the war didn't get over soon, a whole lot of offspring would be missing from school.

Nate and Jed did not want the whole Baptist building to disappear. But they did think it would be just fine, however, if the Lord would cut off the fellows who had poisoned the sorrel gelding and keep them from poisoning the rest of the stock. Such thoughts flew between them as Parson Swift delivered an ear-shattering message that certainly could be heard by the Baptists.

The boys were relieved when the sermon finally ended and they sang the doxology. Standing at the door to greet his parishioners, Parson Swift extended his gnarled hand to Emily as she passed by.

"I was expecting the whole of the Union Army to be in church with you today, Sister Dawson. Have you left them back at the ranch then?"

"They have not come yet," Emily answered quietly.

"Not come?" He seemed astounded by the news that Emily and the boys had remained alone at the ranch this past week without the protection Pettibone had promised to send. "How have you managed, woman?"

"We take turns through the night." She lay a hand on Jed's shoulder. He stood a little taller. "We each keep a two-hour watch. Most of the stock has been brought in to the near corrals. We've hung lanterns on the fence posts and lit the barn as well."

The parson looked grieved at the news. "Sister Dawson! I do declare! You've managed the week without calling for assistance. Well, well, like the builders of the wall of Jerusalem, we must stand watch and pray! The days are evil. The nights a heap more so. Sister Dawson, you are most welcome to stay here at the parsonage until the soldiers arrive at your place." He placed his hand on Nate's shoulder. "Well, boy, would you like to move to town for a while?"

An instant of excitement passed over the faces of both boys, and then Nate replied quietly, "No, sir. Tom told us we was the men on the place till he and Mont come home again. We ain't leavin'."

Pastor Swift looked surprised and then amused. "Well now." He thumped Nate on the back. "A manly attitude, I'll say. And one your father would be right proud of. But your uncle had not foreseen what happened out your way with the horse and the threat to you. Otherwise he would have made arrangements for you to come to town and stay."

"We are managing fine," Emily said proudly. "Thank you for your concern, but you needn't to worry yourself. I have not slept away from the ranch even one night since Jesse brought me here. And I will not be chased out of my home now. Besides, Deputy Pettibone was sure that soldiers would be sent. Perhaps they've arrived while we've been at church."

The muffled cry that reached Tom's ears from across Sansome was a high squeak, abruptly cut off. Tom looked up and down the wooden-planked street in order to find the source. No one was in sight in either direction on the still January night. The theater crowds had all dispersed, gone home before the thin sliver of moon hung its pale crescent overhead.

Tom had felt like a caged animal in the hotel room where Mont lay sleeping. After several uneventful days in San Francisco, what was supposed to happen next? It seemed as though even staying in a haven for Southern sympathizers like the Tehama House and the message he'd given to the desk clerk were no guarantee that Mont would ever chance across some conspirator whom he'd recognize. The people staying at the Tehama were more likely to sing the praises of Jeb Stuart and Bob Lee than Sherman or Grant, but so what? They were still only pursuing ordinary lives. There had been no knocks on the door, no one hanging around that looked sinister, and no one offering to buy military secrets. Perhaps the escaped spy named *Wilson* was not as hot a commodity as the army had thought?

So Tom had come outside to think. How long would they have to remain on this fruitless quest? Two weeks? Three? What if the "plot" turned out to be no more than the ravings of a few lunatics like the harmless Emperor Norton? The thought made Tom grin wryly to himself in the darkness.

A scuffling sound and another anguished protest froze the smile on his face. It sent Tom's hand to his side where the Colt, now on the bureau upstairs, would have hung. Slapping his palm against his leg in frustration, Tom charged across the street anyway, toward a blackened alley beside the American Theater.

Two dark-clad forms and one in lighter colors twisted and spun in the shadows. As Tom approached, the dimly seen forms resolved themselves into rough, drunken men and a panicked, desperate woman.

One man held the woman around the waist with one arm while his other hand was clamped across her mouth.

The second attacker, smaller in height than the first, tried to catch the woman's legs. The men struggled to carry her a few steps farther into the darkness of the alley. Lunging and kicking, the woman partially freed herself and the threesome spun and clattered again in a blur of rustling petticoats and coarse oaths.

Charging straight into the group, Tom tackled the smaller man in a headlong rush that drove both past a stage door and into a brick wall that stood across the middle of the passage. The man's head connected with the masonry with a satisfying crack, and Tom dropped him and whirled around.

The second assailant flung the girl aside. From beneath his dark blue coat he drew a knife with a blade that seemed to be a foot long. "You better go, mister," the man breathed hoarsely. "You hadn't ought to butt into Grove Kinnock's business, unless you's fixin' to meet your Maker."

Tom circled warily, palms open. He kept his eyes on the knife-hand of his opponent.

Tom feinted toward Kinnock, hoping to draw a rush that would give the woman an opportunity to flee. But the knife-wielder was too wary for that, and he stayed an arm's length from the woman, brandishing the tapering blade drunkenly toward Tom's face.

"Cut you good, I aim to," sneered Kinnock. Behind Tom, the smaller man groaned and stirred.

Now the struggle was reaching a critical stage. No doubt the second attacker also had a knife, and from the sounds, he would soon be awake enough to use it. Tom would be caught between the two, still without a means to free the girl.

His boot brushed over a hard, lumpy object—a loose cobblestone or broken chunk of brick. Tom stooped quickly to retrieve it; anything to even the odds.

Tom's fingers had just touched the stone when Kinnock attacked. Shouting "Grab him, Rafe" to his still prostrate accomplice, he lunged toward Tom with a vicious swipe of the dirk.

The point of the blade caught the sleeve of Tom's denim jacket and slit it up to the elbow as he flung himself backward. A second slash of steel followed as a backhand arc at eye level passed within an inch of Tom's face.

Seizing the chance while Kinnock's guard was open, Tom swung the chunk of rock into the side of the man's head. Now it was Grove Kinnock's turn to jump awkwardly aside, but not before the brick had grazed his temple, splitting the scalp and leaving blood dripping from his hair.

"Run!" Tom shouted at the woman, who was still in a tumbled heap of petticoats on the slimy stones. "Run!" he commanded urgently.

With the blow, Kinnock's rage was up. For the moment, he forgot the girl. What he wanted was the chance to drive his blade into Tom's belly; to leave this foolish, interfering stranger gasping out the ebbing of his life.

His alcoholic clumsiness burned away by his anger, Kinnock curled into a fighting crouch. He advanced on Tom with the lightly balanced tread of a man used to the rolling deck of a ship.

"I'm gonna slit you from jib to mizzen," he hissed. "An' when I'm through, I'm gonna feed you to the fish piece by piece."

Tom was silent, standing a pace out from the wall and throwing a quick glance toward Rafe, who was on his knees, struggling to stand. *Why doesn't the girl run? Is she hurt or knocked unconscious?*

The moment for pondering flashed by as Kinnock's stalking approach brought him again within striking range. Though he was enraged, Kinnock was wary of the stone club Tom held aloft in his right hand. He had already suffered a stinging blow, and now moved toward his prey cautiously.

Kinnock lunged with the point of his knife held straight ahead, like a sword thrust. As Tom jumped aside, the sailor turned the movement into a sickle's sweep, expecting to catch Tom in the side.

Tom chopped downward with the improvised club. Using the stone like the primitive ax of an ancient tribesman, Tom snapped his elbow taut, speeding the impact of the jagged edge against Kinnock's forearm.

There was an audible crunch as Kinnock's arm shattered. A howl of pain and a clatter followed as the dirk fell from his nerveless fingers.

Bending swiftly to try and retrieve the knife, Tom caught an upraised knee on the point of his chin. Hundreds more stars than could actually be seen in Frisco's foggy skies exploded in front of his sight. He staggered back, shaking his head to try and clear his vision, but only setting off more cascades of meteors.

Tom could hear Kinnock cursing and scrabbling in the

debris with his uninjured arm. The sailor stood slowly, holding the knife again, his broken arm cradled against his chest.

"I can stick you just as easy . . . with my . . . other hand," he panted. "Rafe," he called, "catch hold of this fella for me. I'm gonna gut him like a sea bass."

The smaller man was up now and staggering forward. Tom still held the stone club, but there was little he could do with it against two. Kinnock blocked the exit and Rafe was closing in.

There was one chance. Rafe still looked unsteady on his feet and Kinnock favored his injured arm. If Tom could maneuver himself behind Rafe, keep the smaller man between him and Kinnock's knife thrusts—

When Kinnock sprang again, Tom flung himself toward Rafe instead. The smaller man did not expect to be attacked and gave ground suddenly. The force of Kinnock's wild slash spun him around out of position.

Tom pressed his rush toward Rafe and had the man by the coat lapels. Swinging him around, Tom prepared to throw him into Kinnock when . . . Tom's feet slipped on the damp pavement and he and Rafe tumbled down together.

Over and over they rolled, thrashing in the alley. They fetched up against the brick wall again.

Kinnock moved into position like a victorious spider, towering overhead. He held the long-bladed knife, point downward, like an ice pick.

"Good," he growled. "Hold him there, Rafe. I'm gonna poke his eyes out, and *then* gut him!" The knife was drawn back to end the battle when—

The explosion of a pistol shot in the narrow confines of the brick canyon sounded like mortar fire. The thunderous roar deafened Tom to all but the reverberating beat of the echoes dying away.

Kinnock was flung back against the wall as if a giant windstorm had thrown him there. Like garments blown from a Telegraph Hill clothesline, he stood propped against the wall, motionless and stiff. An instant later, as a dying breeze releases its stolen prizes, he slumped into a heap.

"Grove? Grove!" shouted Rafe, kicking himself free of Tom. The depth of his concern for his friend evaporated, and he ran out of the alley and down California Street. The tromp of his footsteps on the plank roadway echoed hollowly. The slowly diminishing sounds of his headlong retreat showed that he was still running after blocks and blocks.

The woman came to stand beside Tom. "Did you do that?" he asked, gesturing toward the lifeless Kinnock.

"Yes," she said simply, "with this," and she handed Tom a two-shot derringer, still warm from the explosion of its first charge.

"Ma'am, I . . ." he began, but she took his arm and pulled him toward the street.

"Someone will have heard the shot and the police will come to investigate," she said. "It will be much simpler for us to leave now. Please," she begged, "I promise I'll explain. My hotel is just across the street."

By the lobby light that spilled out on the street as the woman entered, Tom could see that she was startlingly beautiful. Dark ringlets of hair fell in disarray over the shoulders of the evening cloak she wore.

She was tall and her disheveled clothes did not conceal her feminine figure silhouetted against the interior light. Tom allowed her to enter first, alone, as she had requested.

Shortly after, Tom also entered the Tehama House lobby. He wondered if all their caution was necessary. No one had come to investigate the gunshot, and the night clerk was dozing behind the counter.

Her room was 2-B, up one flight and immediately next to the stairs. The door opened quickly at Tom's quiet tap, and she drew him into the room with a nervous glance down the empty corridor.

"Ma'am, I only came to see that you were all right," Tom began awkwardly. "I'll go on now—"

"Please wait," she insisted. "I want to thank you for coming to help me. It was a very brave thing you did."

Tom shuffled his feet and stared down at the roses woven into the carpet. He was trying to avoid looking at the expanse of creamy throat that appeared above the opening of her silk dressing gown. "It seems to me that I should be thanking you," he mumbled.

"Nonsense," she laughed. A slight tremor in her voice betrayed that she was not as entirely in control as she wanted to appear. "Those brutes! I dropped my pistol in the struggle before you appeared. If you had not arrived when you did, they would have . . ."

Tom cleared his throat and again acted as if leaving as soon as possible would please him.

"Please sit," she insisted, and she seated herself on a

mahogany divan whose needlepoint cushions matched the carpet. Tom obliged her by perching stiffly in a straight-backed chair near the door. The air seemed filled with an exotic aroma—the scent of a flower garden blooming in the dead of winter.

"My name is Belle Boyd," she said, pausing as if Tom should recognize it immediately. When he made no comment, she continued. "I'm an actress. I stayed late in the theater tonight, studying lines for a new role. Since the theater is just across the street, I wasn't worried about coming out alone. But those two men! They were right outside the stage door and grabbed me when I stepped out!"

"Why didn't you want the police, ma'am? You could have described the second man. Perhaps they could have caught him."

"That's why I felt I had to explain," she said. "You know that those two men were sailors—*Yankee Navy sailors,*" she spat, as if repeating especially harsh and distasteful swear words. "My sympathies are well-known and clearly with the Confederacy—I would not have received justice. Not after having killed one of *them.* No, it's better this way."

CHAPTER 9

The morning after his first encounter with Belle Boyd, Tom and Mont sat in the dining room of the Tehama House having breakfast. Looking out the window toward the street, the two took in the porticoed veranda and wrought-iron scrollwork by which the builder conveyed an air of Southern gentility.

A lilting voice at their elbows made them turn abruptly. "This view always puts me in mind of Atlanta. Don't you think so, Mr. Wilson?"

Both males jumped to their feet. "Ah, um, Miss Boyd . . . I'm sure the resemblance is exact, if you say so," stammered Tom.

The Cupid's bow of a mouth parted into a smile that included Mont. "What an adorable boy. What is his name, Mr. Wilson?"

Mont took an instant dislike to the dark-haired woman, beautiful and friendly though she was. Miss Emily had never spoken *about* him as if he were not present. And besides, what right did this person have to be so familiar with Tom? They had only met the night before.

"This is Mont, Miss Boyd. Mont, make your manners to Miss Boyd," Tom directed.

Mont bowed stiffly from the waist and said in a too quiet, brittle-sounding voice, "Pleased to meet you, ma'am."

"Delightful!" Belle enthused. "So well trained. Have you had him long?"

At least this was a question Tom and Mont had rehearsed. "Oh yes," Tom replied, "and his family before him."

"How nice," Belle responded, but it was plain from her tone and the gaze which she fixed on Tom that her interest in Mont had evaporated, if any had really ever existed. "May I join you?"

"Please," agreed Tom, signaling to a white-coated waiter passing by with a silver coffee pot.

When both adults were seated, Mont, who was still standing, said in a voice that was over-loud this time, "Marse Wilson, shall I go up an' check on your laundry?"

Puzzled by the abrupt departure, Tom agreed rather than asking in front of Belle for an explanation of this contrivance. After Mont was gone and the waiter had poured two fresh cups of coffee, Belle launched into another lengthy thank you for Tom's role in the events of the night before.

"It isn't necessary to thank me," said Tom, looking into the dark brown eyes that held his from across the table. "I could not have done anything else."

"But I am *so* grateful," purred Belle. "Besides, I sense a real kinship of spirit with you. You *are* the Wilson who rescued that dear little editor from those criminal soldiers?"

Tom acknowledged the event with a nod. "Nothing to brag about. I could not let the good man be lynched, even though he acted the part of a fool. There are more effective methods of dealing with Yankees than deriding them in public. But tell me, how do you know that story?"

Belle's chin tilted toward the dining room ceiling as a peal of bell-like laughter bubbled from her throat. "Why Mr. Wilson," she said with mock sternness, "I'm surprised at you! A gentleman never asks a lady to reveal her sources!

"But since you are *that* Wilson, I don't mind telling you," she continued in a conspiratorial tone. She extended her gloved hand across the table toward Tom's coffee cup and wrapped her long, slender fingers around his sturdy, tanned fist. She pulled his hand toward her side of the table with a surprisingly strong grip, and Tom leaned in until their heads almost touched.

"There are still a few true sons of the South in this state," she murmured, "but not nearly enough that a gallant hero like yourself can go unnoticed or unremarked."

A whiff of the same exotic perfume Tom had noticed in Belle's room hit his senses. For an instant the clatter of crockery and the bustle of the waiters disappeared. It felt as if he and Belle were alone together. The two were eye to eye, only a breath apart.

The reverie was interrupted when a dark-suited man walked over to their table and stood alongside. Tom first noticed the pointed toes on the black leather shoes, then scanned upward to the pointed beard and the brooding eyes below the heavy dark brows.

Unhurriedly, Belle leaned back in her chair and said in a completely conversational tone, "As I was saying, Mr. Wilson, your actions have not gone unreported. The fact of the matter is that Mr. Perry here would also like to congratulate you."

Once again, Tom stood and the two men shook hands. Perry had still not said anything. His eyes seemed to try and penetrate Tom's, and his expression was sharp, even harsh. He squeezed Tom's hand with a grip far stronger than courtesy suggested.

If that's how you want it, thought Tom, *I'll play along,* and he returned the crush of the handshake, pound for pound. Belle watched the contest of strength with undisguised amusement.

The first indication that either man was faltering occurred when Perry unlocked his stare and glanced down at his hand. The tips of his fingers had turned white up to the second joints. An involuntary grunt escaped his tightly clenched jaws.

Tom immediately relaxed his grip and gestured with his free hand toward Mont's empty chair. "Please have a seat, Mr. Perry."

"Sturdy handshake," Perry remarked gruffly. Then, as if remembering Belle's introduction, he continued in a friendlier tone, "It's fortunate that a man of your strength was around to come to my fiancée's assistance."

Tom's glance at Belle saw her momentarily flustered, but she recovered her composure quickly. A faint pink tinge lingered as evidence of her discomfort.

Perry draped his arm possessively across the back of Belle's chair. "The Yankee tyrant Lincoln, with his army of invaders, thinks that he can tread on the rights of sovereign states with impunity. Thankfully, courageous men like Garrison still stand up and spit in his eye! But the wheels of oppression are grinding harder and harder. Brave men are fighting and dying for want of assistance. We dare not stand idly by."

Tom's thought ran from how much like a prepared speech this sounded to how ironic it was for a cause that endorsed slavery to speak of being oppressed.

"I have heard similar sentiments expressed before," commented Tom with an air of cautious approval.

"Stronger, Mr. Wilson, stronger! You may speak your mind freely here—you're among friends! You were already vouched for, but your recent actions not only underline your character, but place me personally in your debt. How may I improve your stay in San Francisco?"

Tom's look around the room paused briefly on nearby diners, judging whether the conversation had been over-heard. His prolonged stare at a bald-headed man seated alone at a corner table caused both Perry and Belle to follow his gaze.

As if satisfied at last that he could proceed safely, Tom replied to Jasper Perry's offer. "I have been sent," he said with a note of mystery, "to offer myself to an extremely important effort to aid a glorious cause—at any cost." These words were part of a formula explained to Tom by Colonel Mason.

Perry's expression did not change. In an off-hand way he said to Belle, "I'm sorry you have to leave, my dear. Thank you for your kind introduction." Perry stood and helped the actress up from her chair.

Belle looked nonplussed at the abrupt dismissal, but offered no argument. "I'm sure I won't miss anything but boring man talk and speech making," she said with a flutter of her eyelashes. Then to Tom she said, "Don't believe *everything* he says, Mr. Wilson. Mr. Perry is prone to exaggeration." After this small act of defiance, Belle took her leave. It was clear from the way she bestowed smiles and hellos around the tables that Belle understood the power of her charms.

Both men followed her out of the room with their eyes. At last Perry spoke. "Your arrival could not be more for-tunate. We need to move quickly and decisively."

"You are the leader of the castle, of course," observed Tom. "I knew it immediately."

Perry shook his head with a self-deprecating shrug. "No, not me. I am only a messenger—a foot soldier, if you will. But I'd like you to accompany me to meet our general."

"When?"

"Tonight."

In a carriage with drawn shades, Tom was taken on a roundabout drive through San Francisco. When the ride was over, he was hustled into a warehouse.

"Greetings, Brother Wilson," said a breathy and muffled voice from someone in a throne-like chair with a mask over his face. Tom took his seat in a circle of four men.

"As you see," Jasper Perry explained in rather unctuous tones, "we are small in number, but not in courage. Many have abandoned our cause because of cowardice or personal greed, but those who remain are undoubted. You have shown yourself to be worthy of our trust."

Perry continued, "We need your help on an important matter. We want you to join forces with some brothers in Virginia City, Nevada Territory. Will you go?"

"What am I to do there?" Tom asked.

"That will be explained at the proper time," Perry responded. "All you must do for now is take a room at the Tahoe Hotel. You will be contacted there. Will you go?"

"Yes, of course," Tom responded, not really certain if he meant to go or not. "But I have business to take care of tomorrow. I can leave the next day."

"Very well," intoned the leader, concluding the discussion. "We appreciate your willingness, Brother Wilson. The others in Virginia City are expecting us to send assistance. When you get to the hotel and register, all you need to do is put this word—CHAPMAN—after your name. You'll be contacted. Now, if you'll wait in the next room for just a minute. . . ."

After Tom had left the room, the tone turned less formal. "Do Ingram and Hastings really need his help?" one man asked.

"Ingram has grit; he will stick. But Hastings is young and sometimes soft. He may need to be replaced."

"But what do we really know about this man?"

"We have the description of what he looks like and the report of his escape. We know that he is brave and has shown himself able and willing to stand up to the Yankees. Besides, let me add that Miss Boyd will also be going to the Comstock shortly after. She will keep an eye on him as well. If need be, she can do more than charm him."

The sidewheeler *Yosemite* was just easing into the docks when Tom and Mont approached the wharf. The tall black smokestack towered over the paddlewheels and the walking-beam amidships, dwarfing the pilot house. But the flag of the United States waving bravely at the stern stood out plainly above the gleaming white ship.

"Isn't that a grand sight, Mont?" Tom asked.

" 'Deed it is," agreed Mont. "Mighty proud!"

"You know," Tom added, "if we go to the Comstock like Perry and the secesh want, that boat, or one like it, is how we'll travel up river."

Mont's eyes grew as big as saucers. "You means we'd go 'cross the bay on it?" he asked. The *Yosemite* seemed to sense his enthusiasm and responded by announcing its arrival with a great blast of its steam whistles.

"Not just across the bay, but clear to Sacramento. From there the stage company runs to Virginia City, Nevada Territory." In an afterthought he added, "Of course, from Sacramento you could catch a stage back home, too. Yes sir, just two days from where we're standing and we'd be home." He sounded as if he wished that were the journey being planned, instead of one going farther away.

"Is we goin' to Virginia City for shore?"

"I don't know. I want to ask some advice from the two military men Colonel Mason mentioned to me. I'm afraid if I don't agree to go, then it will look suspicious to Perry and his group. But if I do go, I'm worried about taking you along. The Comstock is plenty rough at the best of times."

Mont started to protest that he'd be just fine, but Tom continued, "You know, if I had any good place to leave you, I'd have you stay here till I got back. I just don't know who with."

Mont's mouth closed with a snap. He'd already decided that the sooner this subject got changed, the better.

They spotted the man Tom had come to see outside an office near the South Beach Ship Yard. Commander Fry was an imposing figure, as tall as Tom and nearly as muscular, despite his sixty years of age. He had a shock of white hair and impressive white burnsides.

His uniform, all brass and braids, included a sword. Mont thought the commander looked a lot like woodcuts he had seen of Andrew Jackson.

"Commander Fry?" Tom confirmed. "My name is

Wilson. I believe Colonel Mason may have mentioned my name to you."

"Wilson, of course. Come in," Fry said tersely. Then to a man dressed in greasy coveralls who had been receiving rapid-fire instructions, he concluded, "I want them here tomorrow. Tomorrow, understand? Not one day later or by thunder I'll have a new foreman."

"Yes sir, Admiral," said the worker in an Irish brogue. "Come sunup tomorrow, they'll be here. It'll be a grand sight, to be sure." The man pulled on his forelock and backed away.

Fry drew Tom and Mont into a small office that contained only one chair and a desk overflowing with plans and blueprints. He did not seat himself, so all three stood in the tiny space. "Wilson," he said again, "heard from Mason. Think it's poppycock. This conspiracy. Anyway, no time to play games. Too busy already."

"Well, sir," said Tom with rising indignation, "Colonel Mason has reason to think there is truth to it and I have already met—"

"Some secesh die-hards? Rubbish," Fry said abruptly. "Good luck to you, Mr. Wilson. What we're about here is more important than chasing fairies. Now if you'll excuse me," and he ushered them out and shut his door.

"Come on, Mont," Tom said, thrusting his hands into his pockets and walking with such angry strides that Mont had to run to keep up. "Let's go see if the Army treats us any better. If nobody wants to give us the time of day, maybe we'll just go home."

CHAPTER 10

The path leading down the hill toward Fort Point took Tom and Mont past the commander's house. They knocked, but no one answered.

The commander of Fort Point's garrison of two hundred men lived in a small frame house, freshly painted white and trimmed in forest green. It stood on a knoll just above the brick fortress. From the yard beside the home, the soldiers on guard duty atop the walls of the fort could be seen patrolling their posts.

A northwest wind funnelled past the Marin headland and made the flag waving over the casements snap on its halyard. It was a pleasant day for an outing to view the Golden Gate, the entrance to the greatest natural harbor in the world.

But if the scene from the knobby hill was inspiring and enjoyable, descending the wooden staircase to stand in the shadow of the three-story-high citadel brought back the reality of war. Soldiers were drilling on the cleared area in front of the fort's single entrance. They marched and counter-marched under the critical eye of a red-bearded sergeant-major. He gave them the benefit of his opinion at every opportunity, expressed in a voice that resounded from the brick walls and rocky cliffside with such volume that Tom thought it must be heard in Sausalito across the bay.

Tom and Mont heard him question a soldier's intellect, morals, upbringing and ancestry when the man had failed to execute "order arms" properly. When the sergeant-major saw Tom and Mont approaching, he must have decided that another opportunity for a lesson had presented itself. He pointed to three soldiers and waved them forward.

"Kirby, Seldon, Morris—you three are the guard detail. Kirby is acting corporal. Let me see you make a proper challenge and report."

"Halt! Who goes there?" demanded the one named Seldon, pointing a bayonet at Tom's midsection.

"Corporal 'the guard! Post number one!" shouted Morris.

"Escort the uh, the uh—" Kirby stumbled, uncertain if these were prisoners or visitors. The glare he received from Sergeant-Major Donovan would have melted one of the antique bronze cannons that flanked the entrance.

Under Donovan's withering stare, Kirby swallowed hard and reported. "Corporal 'the guard, Sergeant-Major. Post number one is escorting two unknown persons."

Donovan puffed out his whiskers like a surfacing sea lion and advanced past where Kirby stood quivering at attention.

"Sergeant-Major Donovan," he announced to Tom. "What is your name and purpose?"

"My name is Wilson," said Tom, "and this is Mont. We are here to see Captain Tompkins."

"Regrettably, sir, Captain Tompkins is ill and in the hospital. Lieutenant Reynolds is in command."

"I see," said Tom with some consternation. "Would you please ask the lieutenant if he will see me? My business here was suggested by Colonel Mason of Fort Tejon."

"Of course. If you will wait here, please."

In a brief space of time, Donovan was back and now offered to escort Tom and Mont to Reynolds' office himself. As they passed into the interior of the fort, the high walls shut out the sunlight and sound with the finality of a prison cell door.

Lieutenant Reynolds was a plump, soft-looking young man, about Tom's age. He had a receding chin but a prominent nose that he was fond of looking down, as though sighting a cannon. He affected the dress uniform of the artillery, including a red sash and black ostrich-plumed hat.

After introductions, Tom proceeded to explain his real identity and his reason for being in San Francisco with Mont. "So you see," he summarized, "Colonel Mason believed that the plot was real enough to bear investigation and that Mont might recognize one of the principals."

"And has he?" Reynolds inquired, aiming his nose at Mont.

"No," Tom said, "but *I* may have stumbled on to something." He went on to describe Jasper Perry and the mysterious meeting that called for him to make a trip to the Comstock.

When he had finished, Reynolds leaned back in his chair and laced his pudgy fingers together. "There may be some real importance to what you have uncovered, and I want you to know I take it seriously. But we must proceed slowly and carefully. It would not do to spook one bird and let the covey escape. Are you agreeable to going to Virginia City to see if you can discover the others in the plot?"

"Yes, except that I dislike dragging Mont all over the countryside. Besides, it could be dangerous for him. But I think the gang will be suspicious if I don't go."

"Acting reluctant at this point would certainly raise some questions," Reynolds agreed. "How about this: Mont can stay with me while you make a rapid trip there to see what you can discover, then return on some pretext, and we'll round up all of them you can identify."

"Leave Mont with you?" Tom said a little dubiously.

"Would you rather that we arrest this actress—what's her name, Boyd, for questioning? See what information we can get from her?"

"No, no," said Tom hastily. "You're right that we should know more first. We don't want to tip off the others."

"Splendid," said Reynolds. "You can leave Mont with me now and send his things back. Will you be leaving tonight?"

Tom looked over at Mont and thought he saw a tear forming in the corner of the boy's eye. "No," he said quickly, "we have some important business tonight, Mont and I. Why don't you come and pick him up at our hotel, Tehama House, tomorrow at ten, if that's all right. I'll leave on the noon steamer."

"Excellent," agreed Reynolds. "Now come and let me show you around the fort. Mont, you will see that it will be fun to stay here." To Tom he added, "And you will see how foolish it is to think of any Confederate attempt to seize this position. By the way, I think it's best if you say nothing to anyone else about the plot. You can't tell who might be secesh in this town."

Their footsteps echoed hollowly as he led the way up dark staircases. They emerged on the highest level of the fort. Walking over to a row of cannons, Reynolds patted one affectionately, as if it were a prize horse in a show ring. "Sixty-eight pounder," he said proudly. "Columbiad with a rifled barrel. This weapon can propel a shot two miles or more. The one hundred and twenty of these command more than a half circle on the entrance to the bay."

"What's this?" asked Mont, pointing at a brick and cast-iron contraption with a chimney.

"Furnace," observed Reynolds, "for heating shells red-hot."

"This is all very impressive," commented Tom. "But what if the garrison were surprised and the guns seized? After all, these guns all face the water."

"True enough," agreed Reynolds, "but we have field pieces and mortars to defend the landward side, and two full companies of troops."

Tom and Mont prepared to take their leave then, after thanking Reynolds for showing them around. "Not at all, not at all," he concluded. "I'll see you both tomorrow."

He and Tom conversed quietly for a few more minutes, then Mont and the rancher from Shadow Ridge left the fort.

Halfway up the hill again, the man and the boy turned to view the harbor channel one more time. A Pacific mail steamer was bustling into the Gate, churning a streaming wake of white foam and a double trail of black smoke. She passed an outbound square-rigged sailing ship and the two exchanged salutes—steam whistle screaming a reply to the sharp report of a swivel cannon.

Both ships dipped pennants by way of respect to the American flag flying over the fort. A thirty-two pounder roared a reply. It seemed also to be a reminder of how strong and solid the Union defenses of the bay really were.

Tom stood with his hand on Mont's shoulder and both took in the panorama of the scene. "I can't understand how Perry and the others can be so confident," Tom said, half to himself. "Maybe they *are* crazy."

"I 'spect they see somethin' we doesn't see," Mont suggested.

In the glow of the lantern light, Jed looked older than his eleven years. He perched in the hayloft with his father's old Greener shotgun across his lap. At Emily's footstep on the threshold of the barn, he challenged, "Who's that there?"

"Ma," she answered, struck by the manliness of his young voice. "I've brought you another blanket. Some milk and bread with butter and sugar." She stood at the bottom of the ladder as he peered over and then climbed down to retrieve the tin lunch bucket. "You let me know if you get too tired and I'll take the watch," she offered.

He replied with an indignant snort. "I ain't little no more like Nate. I can take his watch and yours as well, if I need to. Nobody's gonna get past that barn door unless I give 'em permission."

She did not ask him if he was ever frightened. To do so would have been an insult. Nor did she admit that a dozen times throughout her own watch she had felt the chill of fear at the rustling sounds in the night. An owl hooting in the oak tree, the restless stirring of the horses in the corral at the side of the barn, had tightened her grip on the stock of the gun and turned calm prayers into a torrent of frightened entreaties to the Almighty for protection.

No doubt Jed had felt the same. Little Nate had fled into the house and now could not stand his watch alone anymore. Jed simply slept beside him in the hay throughout Nate's watch. A dozen times Nate woke him with a shake and the frantic question, *"You hear that?"* After his watch, Nate would stumble into the house and Jed would shake himself awake to sit alone for another two hours.

"You're doing fine, son," Emily said with genuine admiration. "Just remember when you're tired, the Lord never sleeps nor slumbers. He is keeping watch over us in ways we cannot see."

Jed nodded and sipped his milk. "I just wish He'd send us some soldiers to help out. I mean blue-coated soldiers that I could see." A wry smile crossed his lips. A smile so much like his father's.

"They're bound to come." She looked at the animals in the stalls and wondered if perhaps the Union soldiers did in fact consider guarding the Dawson ranch a trivial matter. Too unimportant to deal with. She did not express her doubt to Jed, however. "In the meantime, it's just us. And no doubt great armies of angels all around us. Enough for now or there would be others here as well."

He nodded and glanced up toward the loft. One hand on the ladder and then he froze.

Far away in the darkness the sound of hoofbeats echoed on the rock-hard roadbed. Jed shoved the bucket into his mother's arms and scrambled up the ladder to retrieve the shotgun. "Get to the house," he instructed her in manly tones. "They're still aways off. Get the rifles and the revolver."

Emily ran to the house, wishing that there were soldiers of the blue-coated sort right now to help them! The hoofbeats came nearer, turning onto the lane that led to the ranch house. She took the Winchester from the gun rack and wrested the Colt revolver from its holster. Asleep on the sofa, Nate stirred, groaned, and rolled over to settle into a deeper sleep. It was good that he was unaware of her own sense of fear, Emily thought. Then a renewed anger flooded her as she thought of Tom Dawson off chasing shadows when there was such a real and terrible threat right here at home! When were those soldiers coming? And when would Tom be back? She would give him a piece of her mind when he showed up!

She carried the kerosene lantern outside with her and put it on the tree stump beside the hitching rail. Then she stepped back in the shadows to wait as the riders came near. The Dawson family had rehearsed this plan several times.

"I'm here, Jed," she called loudly. "I've got the guns!" She hoped the riders would hear the threat in her voice and turn around. They did not.

"We got 'em covered, Ma," Jed called bravely. No doubt he too hoped to discourage whoever was coming.

It was then that a familiar voice rang out from the darkness of the lane. "Sister Dawson! Young Jed! Do not shoot! It is Parson Swift here! I've brought my sons along to stand watch with you tonight!"

CHAPTER 11

Awake and looking out the window, Mont watched the misty fingers of fog just beginning to relinquish their grip on the street lamps. Today Mont would go to stay with the lieutenant at Fort Point, but right now he was waiting in the room at the Tehama Hotel.

Tom had left long before daylight. After checking steamer sailings from Frisco and stage connections from Sacramento to Virginia City, Tom had decided on the early departure. "I can save a whole day's wait in Sacramento this way," he explained to Mont. "Don't worry. I'll be back soon and Lieutenant Reynolds will look after you."

The lieutenant had wanted Mont to stay at the fort last night, but Tom had insisted that he and Mont have dinner together and take in a show at the Melodeon Theater. Besides, Tom had suggested to Reynolds that Mont could point out secesh conspirators around the hotel. Reynolds had agreed. He would come in civilian clothes in the morning to pick up Mont. His Army uniform would certainly frighten the rebels, and it could be disastrous if a Union officer were seen talking with Tom and Mont.

Even without the lieutenant's red sash and ostrich plume hat, Mont now spotted the officer coming up the street. Reynolds paused to strike a match on a lamppost and lit his cigar. He was wearing a plain, dark-blue cape and a cloth cap.

Mont was already dressed and bounced out of the room to the stairwell in anticipation of Reynolds' arrival. In the silence of the still early morning, Mont could hear the clump of the heavy boots coming up the stairs. Ten steps to the landing and ten more to the second floor, Mont counted. The climbing tread stopped. *That's funny,* Mont thought, *guess he forgot we wuz on three.* Mont leaned over the railing to call down to Reynolds to come up one more flight.

Stretching out above the stairwell, Mont caught a glimpse of a dark blue back and shoulder one floor below. As he watched, a fist rose and fell on the door nearest the steps in two quick knocks, followed by two more.

The door to Miss Boyd's room was opened by Jasper Perry. Reynolds stepped hastily through and the panel was quickly closed behind him.

Something was wrong, very wrong. Why was the Union army officer going to meet with the conspirators? It did not look like he was there to arrest them. Mont had to find out.

He tiptoed quietly down the steps, then looked all around to see if anyone was nearby before placing his ear close to the keyhole. The volume of voices coming from Belle's room was loud enough that Mont did not have to strain to hear:

"What do you mean, he's not one of us!" shouted the voice of Jasper Perry.

"Calm down and lower your voice," demanded Reynolds. "There is no harm done. We'll take care of him the same way we did the other imposter."

"But he's already gone to the Comstock," murmured Belle.

Now it was Reynolds' turn to be surprised. "What?" his voice squeaked. "He wasn't due to leave till noon."

"I saw him off early this morning," said Belle, "on his way to the steamer."

"All right," said Reynolds, back in control. "Belle, you are leaving for the Comstock at once. I won't trust this message to the wire, what with Pinkerton men everywhere. You must see Ingram. Tell him to hire someone outside the circle, but do it quickly!"

"But, General, what about the nigger brat?" Perry wanted to know.

"We'll hang on to him as a hostage till we know the job is done," Reynolds concluded.

"Ho there, you boy," boomed a voice down the hall behind Mont. "What are you sneakin' 'round that door for?" The conversation in the room stopped abruptly and running steps came toward the door.

Mont's headlong flight took him down the stairs three steps at a time. At the bottom he did a neat swing around a wrought-iron bannister and came off the last six steps airborne, flying feet first.

His boots collided with the stomach of a well-dressed, portly, recently fed gentleman. The collision produced an "oof," followed by a groan. The large man revolved slowly like a ship capsizing and sank down on the bottom step, holding his paunch. His girth blocked the stairs and when Mont's pursuers reached the ground floor, they could not get by.

Reynolds made one polite, encouraging noise, asking

the man to move. When Perry saw Mont race past the doorman, he tried to leap over the roadblock . . . unsuccessfully, as it turned out.

The large man had tried to oblige Reynolds by clearing the stairs, and so stood up just as Jasper Perry hurdled over. A kick behind the ear dropped the poor man to the floor again and sent Perry sprawling onto the marble tiles. He partly caught himself on his hands, but not soon enough to keep his forehead from smacking the pavement. He got up looking dazed, and wandered toward the desk clerk.

Running past the jumbled heap of bodies, Reynolds dashed out the front door. He spotted Mont a half block away, running north on Sansome.

At the same time, a policeman turned the corner of Sacramento Street, right in Mont's path. Behind him, Reynolds yelled, "Stop him, he's a pickpocket!" The nine-year-old did not think of trying to explain his side of the story. All he saw was another pair of arms outstretched to grab him. Mont ducked his head one way and threw his body the other. The policeman's arms closed around only empty air.

A bell began to clang behind him in furious alarm. Mont accelerated his pace, terrified at the size of the alarm that was being raised—all of San Francisco must be after him!

The clanging bell was getting closer. It seemed to be chasing him up the street. Everyone on the sidewalks had stopped to watch the pursuit. A pair of ladies in long-skirted dresses and high collars formed a barrier with their folded umbrellas. Mont jumped between them, barely clearing the spiked tips.

He caromed into a man wearing baggy trousers and holding a basket of oranges. The fruit the man had been displaying for sale to passersby spun up in the air and all over the sidewalk. A second later an orange flew past Mont's head, and a stream of angry foreign words like "cochito prieta" and "serpeinto" also pursued his flight.

Now the sounds of a whole cavalry troop chased Mont. His short legs were beginning to tire, but he forced himself to keep them churning, struggling to stay ahead of the army that must be pursuing.

A trio of boys a little older than Mont watched him run toward them. They made no move to step aside, but kept staring back the way he had come as if they could not believe the strength of the chase either!

Mont lowered his head and plowed straight into them. Cries of "Hey, watch out!" and "What'er you tryin' to do!" erupted. Mont was showered with fists and boots, but he kicked free and made a dash to cross Clay Street. The terrible clanging alarm bell and the thundering hooves were right behind. Mont took off from the curb in a jump that would have landed him in the middle of the street—and was tackled from behind by all three boys yelling, "Look out! You're gonna get killed!" as the hook-and-ladder wagon of Engine Company Number Five rattled, pounded, and rumbled around the corner.

The rear of the elongated vehicle careened around the turn, brushing the lamppost that hung over the boys' heads. The iron-shod hooves of the coal-black horses and the iron-rimmed wheels pounded past them only inches away.

"You better watch where you're runnin'!" yelled a tow-headed boy in a cloth cap.

"Yeah," agreed another, "them firemen don't stop for nothin'!"

"What was you runnin' so hard for anyway?" questioned the third, an olive-skinned street urchin with bare feet.

"I was . . ." Mont began, looking fearfully down the street. He spotted Reynolds, puffing and wheezing but still pursuing, two blocks behind. "I gotta go," Mont shouted, jumping up. "Thanks!" And off he went, sprinting around the corner on Clay, following the rapidly disappearing fire wagon with its load of men, ladders and axes.

Setting his sights on a large brick and granite building ahead of him kept Mont from accidentally turning back toward his pursuers. He jogged left, then two rights, and then left again. What he was in search of, he could not have said, except to be far enough ahead to have a chance to hide.

The opportunity just did not present itself. His landmark, when he passed it, turned out to be a bustling collection of businesses with offices of the Alta California newspaper and the Bank Exchange Saloon. The people there were all well-dressed men in business suits, top hats, and frock coats. Mont thought about asking one of them for help. Then he remembered that Jasper Perry was wearing a top hat and a frock coat, so he ran on, turning again toward the west.

When he reached Washington Street, two things changed: the most enormous hill yet reared up in front of him and the nature of the pedestrians altered. As if by magic, the sidewalks were suddenly filled with hundreds of small pigtailed men dressed in dark blue tunic-shirts. Their shirt-tails hung below their waists and the over-long sleeves concealed their hands.

An elderly Chinese man was coming slowly toward Mont. He wore the same flapping shirt and baggy trousers as the rest, but he had a black silk skullcap on his head. He was followed by two lean, angry-looking men who walked five steps behind. They were dressed completely in black, and their eyes were constantly moving from side to side as they scanned alleys, balconies and doorways.

The rising slope of the approach to Nob Hill was too much for Mont's short, tired legs. His scamper slowed to a trot, then to a walk. He was even considering turning around and heading downhill, when he spotted Reynolds, still chasing, behind him again. Mont tried to speed up again, but found he could not. His legs felt like lead.

Reynolds, too, was exhausted. His puffing and wheezing had made it impossible for him to call out for help to any of the passersby. He had tried to shout, "Stop, thief!" and wave his hat in the hopes that some citizen would tackle a supposed pickpocket, but the sound of the fire wagon's passing had eclipsed his strangled yell. After that, he just had not had the breath.

When the lieutenant realized that Mont was leading him up Nob Hill, he knew it was over unless . . . Bending down to a cross-draw holster that hung inside his cape, Reynolds drew an octagonal-barrelled Colt and leaned against a lamppost to steady his aim.

The two bodyguards of the elderly Chinese man saw Reynolds draw his gun. They had no idea why this man would want to kill their boss, but their job was to protect him, no matter what.

From the deep pockets of their black tunics, both men drew short-barrelled Allen pepperboxes and began firing. The range was long and the guns inaccurate even at much closer distance, but their shots made Reynolds throw himself to the ground and hug the base of the post.

As soon as they had fired, the bodyguards dragged their employer into a shop that sold ginseng roots and disappeared with him through its back door. Mont also managed to disappear at the sound of the first shot: he ducked into an alleyway so narrow that two men could not walk side by side.

There was a hole in the pavement of the alleyway. Ten running steps down the passage, the rungs of a wooden ladder protruded two feet above the surface.

Mont grasped the topmost rung and looked into the shadowy darkness below. Then making up his mind as he gathered his courage, Mont dropped quickly off the face of San Francisco and into the depths of Chinatown.

CHAPTER 12

The first thing Mont noticed when he descended into the man-made underground grotto was the incredible variety of smells. Not the dark, or the dirt, although there were plenty of both. It was the strange, almost touchable swirl of aromas assaulting his nose that gave Mont the sense of having dropped into another world.

At first he couldn't quite identify the odors, but somehow they stirred up memories. Sharp but pleasant smells that brought to mind Emily's kitchen: tea. Steamy, starchy air full of reminders of iron kettles in slave quarters: boiling rice. Pepper, oranges, fish—dark smells, bright smells, clean smells, moldy smells, all jumbled in a stew of airborne concoction. Floating through the mix was a too sweet, too heavy aroma of decay . . . the odor of wilted flowers heaped on a grave.

Mont crept along the passageway toward a dimly flickering lantern. Beneath it, the corridor came to an intersection. Three underground roads led off in different directions.

The tunnel that went straight ahead had no features to distinguish it from the other two, but Mont chose it in order to find his way back to the ladder and the outside air. Another lantern in the distance provided a new goal as the tiny square of sunlight dwindled and finally disappeared.

A room opened beside the next lantern. It was a low-ceilinged cavern packed with narrow, wooden bunks like the crews' quarters on ships. These bunks were only five feet long and were stacked five deep, with little more than one foot of space between them. At first Mont thought the room was empty, but his ears told him otherwise: some of the bunks were occupied with gently snoring sleepers.

A soft padding sound like that a cat makes walking on a hardwood floor caused Mont to turn around quickly. Mont faced a pair of pajama-coated Chinese, whom he had not even heard till they were three feet behind him.

When they spotted Mont lurking in the doorway, both men burst into excited questions and accusations. Though Mont could understand no word of their talk, the meaning was plain: "What are you doing here?" "You don't belong here!" "Go away at once!"

Mont dashed off again, deeper into the darkness. Erupting from a lighted side passage ahead, a blast of steam shot into the corridor as if an Oriental dragon's lair shared the tunnel.

The chatter of voices slowed Mont's travel. He listened, trying to sort out the meaning of the repeated rubbing, thumping, and splashing noises. Slowly he went up to the doorway and peered in. It was an underground laundry. Pigtailed workers stripped to the waist amid clouds of steam and the vapors of soap, starch, and bluing were boiling copper cauldrons full of clothes, which they stirred with long wooden paddles. Near a wooden staircase leading up stood a thin man with sharp angles to his face. He was dressed all in black and he kept apart from the workers' conversations.

The staircase looked promising. To be able to pop back out of this rabbit warren a different way than he entered seemed like a good plan. But would the Chinese notice him? Would they let him pass?

The question was answered as soon as Mont appeared inside the room. None of the workers saw him, but the man in black certainly did. Raising a yell that could not mean anything other than "Get him!" Mont again found himself pursued, this time by a half-dozen Orientals. *How can everybody be in on trying to catch me?* he wondered. *Two hours ago, nobody was after me.*

Mont turned to flee the laundry, but met with a greater problem. His desire to get out of the underground world was blocked by the approach of more shouting Chinese voices, so he had no choice but to plunge still deeper into the maze.

And maze it had become. At the next intersection Mont took the path toward the right and almost immediately came to another branching choice. This time the fork was not a straight line at all, but a sinuous, winding curve. Several times it came to dead ends or blind corners that required hasty backtracking. Twice he had to duck under a low doorway and twice more he had to jump up and climb over a brick partition.

It was as if someone had built that passageway to be deliberately difficult to follow. The sounds of his pursuers dropped further and further back and presently died away altogether.

Mont glimpsed a light up ahead. He prayed that it would be a way out, but still he approached it with caution.

The light came through a doorway blocked by a wrought-iron grate. Mont could see a room beyond the grate, but could not tell if it was occupied. The boy stifled a cough as the sticky, sweet decayed flower aroma that pervaded the whole underground suddenly increased a hundred times.

Creeping up to the grate, Mont peered through. It was a dimly lit room with walls painted in dark red. Near the center of the room burned a small coal fire on a short round stand.

Shifting behind the grate, Mont changed his angle to

see as much of the room as he could. Built against the wall opposite was a series of bunks, much like the ones Mont had seen earlier, only these were covered in black lacquer and had curtains that could be drawn across the openings.

Mont jerked back into the shadows as a moving form appeared in the room. A wizened man, whose sallow face sagged with the weight of his years, padded noiselessly into the room. His pigtail was yellowed with age, and his wispy yellow chin-whiskers divided into two long strands that hung down on his green silk brocade robe.

The figure bent over a clay jar that was emblazoned with intertwined red and gold dragons. From it he extracted a tiny quantity of something on the tip of a long blackened fingernail. He rolled the substance between forefinger and thumb, then inserted it deftly into the tiny bowl of a short brass-bowled pipe from a rack near the fire.

A glowing splinter of wood grasped in one clawed hand and the brass pipe clutched in the other, the ancient man shuffled toward the curtained alcove. "Mista Sims," he called softly. "You likee mo' black smoke?"

From behind the curtain, a croaking groan emerged, followed by, "What . . . what time is it?"

The old man gave a low wheezing chuckle. "Is no time here, Mista Sims. In plenty black smoke is only dreams."

"Blast your eyes!" the croaking voice reviled. "What is the time?"

In a hurt tone, the withered stick of a man responded, "If you no wantee mo' pipe, I take away," and he turned half around from the bunk.

"Wait!" the addict demanded. His hand tore open the

curtain and grabbed the old man roughly by the shoulder. "Give me that pipe!"

"All light, Mista Sims. Takee pipe . . . Here fire . . . good, good. . . ." The man named Sims seized the offered opium pipe and puffed it eagerly, then drew the pipe inside the bunk space and shut the curtain with a long contented sigh.

The old Chinaman returned to squat by the fire. He rubbed his hands together over the coals, then appeared to recall some necessary errand. Slowly straightening to a crooked comma shape, he shuffled toward an unseen exit at the far end of the room and disappeared.

Wincing at the creaking of the rusty iron hinges, Mont pushed on the lattice grate. A thin shriek of protest came from the little-used frame, then it swung open into the room. Mont breathed a sigh of relief: he had been afraid it would be locked.

His head felt funny from the opium smoke that floated around the underground chamber. Mont listened carefully for any sounds of movement, but heard nothing. Even the addict in the bunk had fallen completely silent now. When a chunk of coal collapsed on the brazier into a pile of ash, Mont started nervously. He was ready to dash back into the tunnel, but he controlled the urge, telling himself that the way out of this underground maze lay forward, not back.

At the far end of the room was a doorway, partly concealed by a silk hanging. A stray breath of fresh air somehow found its way down into the opium den, stirring the thin cloth. *Hurry,* it seemed to urge, *get out quickly.*

Mont's headlong rush into the silk curtain made a pair of streamers that flew from his shoulders as he raced through. Like a Chinese kite trailing twin tails as it soars upward, Mont sailed up the incline at top speed. And just as a kite's ascent is halted abruptly when it reaches the end of the string, Mont's progress suddenly stopped as a clawed fist seized him by the arm and demanded, "Where you go, little black child?"

As Mont kicked and flailed his arms trying to free himself, a second ghastly set of fingernails closed around his neck. "You be still," the ancient Chinaman ordered, "or pletty soon I tear throat out!" When Mont complied and stopped struggling, the old man observed, "You no thinkee Wo Sing hear you breathe in tunnel? What you do here?"

He released just enough pressure from the nail points against Mont's windpipe to allow a reply. "Please, sir," Mont begged. "I was just running from some bad men and I come down here to hide. Can you help me?"

The wiry little man gathered both strands of wispy beard in the claw he took off Mont's neck and stroked downward. "Helpee you? Sure, sure. You come with Wo Sing."

The two walked quietly along another twisting passage with the appearance of friendliness, but a threatening hand rested lightly on Mont's shoulder all the time. Presently, they turned a corner to face an alcove watched over by two black-suited guards.

Some discussion in Chinese passed back and forth before the opium den attendant was permitted to take Mont through the doorway. The room beyond the door looked like the descriptions Mont had heard of the throne rooms of kings. The walls were covered with red silk hangings, embroidered with Chinese characters worked in gold. A thick carpet lay underfoot and overhead were round hanging lamps made of pale green glass with brass fittings.

Against one wall sat a group of musicians who seemed to be tuning their strange instruments. When the discordant sounds continued without pause, Mont decided that this was what passed for music among the Chinese. A closer look revealed that Mont could not recognize any of the instruments anyway—no wonder it sounded strange to his ear!

Just as Mont was beginning to enjoy inspecting the alien surroundings, he was shoved hard from behind. "Is not time for gawking," said Wo Sing harshly. Mont was propelled toward a raised platform at the far end of the room.

On the platform sat a Chinese man of indeterminate age. He wore a long cream-colored robe, which Mont thought looked like a night shirt, a dark blue vest trimmed in red, and a pair of round spectacles.

He was smoking a long-stemmed ivory pipe, resting the bowl on his knee as he drew leisurely puffs. Four men sat at a low table just below and to the side of the "throne." They had been eating and talking, but stopped to watch Wo Sing bring Mont forward.

About halfway to the platform, Mont again received a shove from behind, this time throwing him to his knees. Wo Sing got down beside him and hissed, "Knock head! Knock head! Do all same me." Wo Sing proceeded to prostrate himself on the floor, while helping Mont by grabbing a handful of the little boy's tightly curled hair.

Wo Sing then crawled over to the edge of the platform, dragging Mont along with him. Every few feet, he paused to knock Mont's head against the carpet.

The man on the high seat gestured for Wo Sing to speak. A conversation took place in which Mont must have been central, because Wo Sing plucked the boy's sleeve several times and butted his head down to the floor twice more.

When the speaking was finished, Wo Sing again stretched himself on the floor, then began crawling backward toward the door, leaving Mont behind.

"Hey!" Mont called, raising up and looking around. "Where you goin'? Do I get out of here now?"

Never pausing in his backward slither, Wo Sing merely shook his head and replied, "This great master of Sum Yop Tong, Fujing Toy. You belong him, now."

Mont jumped up exclaiming, "Belong? I doesn't *belong* to nobody no more!"

From the shadows at the sides of the room, two more blackshirts rushed forward. They seized Mont and carried him suspended by the arms out of the room through a door behind the platform. Once in another dim passage, they opened a heavy oak door and threw him in.

Reynolds had given up the pursuit and returned to Jasper Perry. "It doesn't matter," he said. "He can't harm us anyway. And if he turns up again, we'll—"

Captain Law burst into the room. His normally wary pale eyes were unusually animated as he waved his bandaged hand wildly. "It's the *Camanche*, I tell you! We've got to move now—now, or it's hopeless."

"Start again, man," Perry urged. "Slowly and from the beginning."

"Whiskey," Law demanded and Perry complied. After swallowing half a water glass full in one gulp, Law visibly took control of his nervousness and tried again to explain. "I was down on the docks, a sizin' up wharf rats for crew, just as ye said. Outside the South Beach Boat Yard I sees a line of men a waitin' at a guard shack . . . hundreds of men, maybe. I like to keep a weather eye on how blows the news, so I sharpen my course toward a likely knot of greasy-lookin' customers. 'Well mates,' I sez, friendly-like, 'what's the scuttlebutt? Are ye shippin' out for China or to go fight the Rebs?' An uncommon hairy one riz up on my port beam an' throws in with, 'We ain't no swabbies, we be mechanics.' "

"So what?" interrupted Reynolds in an exasperated tone. "The boat works has some rich man's yacht to float, no doubt. Probably ten or twelve underpaid jobs."

Law's eyes now snapped with anger as he shook his shock of white hair from side to side in denial. "Put a reef in your mouth and unfurl your ears," he snorted. "The hairy one sez they's hirin' close on *one hundred* men— *iron workers!*"

"Iron workers?" responded Perry incredulously. "What do they think . . ." His voice trailed off uncertainly as an unpleasant thought crossed his mind.

Law nodded vigorously and the white stubble of his three-day-old beard waved in agreement. "Now you catch my drift *and* you can smell the storm on the breeze.

Why *does* a shipyard need iron workers? And why hire up such a mob all at once?"

"Because," Perry said soberly, sitting down abruptly on his bed, "because they are finishing an ironclad—a monitor—right here in San Francisco Bay."

"Dead on! And in a terrible hurry, too. Word is the Navy Department wants this new Ericsson-boat to protect the coastwise shipping against rebel attacks."

"No!" exclaimed Reynolds, a look of horror and betrayal on his face. "How can they know? Where is the traitor?" He shot a murderous look at the sea captain as if he suspected Law of having personally given away their plans for piracy.

"Steady on," Law demanded, helping himself to another glassful of whiskey. "If they knew, they'd be a hirin' police, not mechanics. This be a *pre*-caution, I thinks, and a way to put fear into would-be rebels. How is the temper of *your* metal, anyway?"

Reynolds considered what Law had said and began to regain his composure. "An ironclad here! Soon! This certainly changes things. We will have to move quicker than ever, *and* we will need to capture or destroy that ship, or all our plans will come to nothing. What did you say they call it?"

"*Camanche*," Law replied grimly.

Mont pounded on the cell door, but the dull thuds made by his small fists barely even echoed within the cell. Slowly his eyes adjusted to the darkness until the light from the corridor that outlined the crack around the oak barrier spread into a thin glow by which Mont could examine his prison.

His gaze froze when he discovered he was not alone. In the back corner of the tiny chamber stood a man. Or was he sitting? The figure's head almost touched the ceiling, but the bony projections drawn up in front of him had to be knees. *Impossible!*

"Who are you?" Mont breathed, backing up till his own head brushed the rough timbers of the door.

"Han" was the brief reply.

"Han," Mont repeated. "Is that your name? I is Mont, Mont James. Why is you in here?"

The gaunt-faced man responded slowly, unsure of his words, "I ran from Fujing Toy."

"You mean you was trying to escape? Me, too," said Mont, eager for an ally in this strangely mysterious world.

Han stretched out his knees and his legs extended half the length of the cell.

"Say," Mont marvelled, "how tall is you?"

"Umm, seven feet," the man responded.

"Wow!" Mont exclaimed. "I never seed a Chinaman big as you. Fact is, I thought they was all short fellers. Is you Chinese?"

Han nodded wearily. "Mountain people in China. I brought here as slave for Tong lord Fujing Toy."

"You is big enough to wallop four of them blackshirts," Mont observed. "Next time you'll make it to freedom."

Shaking his head Han replied, "They not feed me . . . I too weak to fight boo-how-doys, blackshirts."

CHAPTER 13

Each evening a different family from Mount Carmel Presbyterian Church arrived at the door of the Dawson ranch. While the men took turns sitting up throughout the night to guard the livestock against unseen threat, the women sewed and the children played upstairs in the loft until bedding down for the night.

What Colonel Mason and the Union Army had not done to protect the Dawsons, the church family had managed nicely. Ranchers who could fervently belt out a hymn or recite a scripture passage by heart now sat with scatter-guns across their laps as they gazed down at dark shadows from the loft in the barn.

Pastor Swift preached that vengeance indeed belonged to the Lord, and the Lord would just as well use a shotgun as a bolt of lightning if any varmint tried to harm the widow Dawson and her young'ins or their stock!

Each morning, men chopped firewood while their women and children fixed breakfast in the Dawson kitchen. With the light of day, the watching ended. Except that Emily continued to watch the road for the return of Tom and Mont, or for the coming of the blue-coated army that Deputy Pettibone had pledged to send.

The next morning (at least Mont supposed it was morning), two small bowls of rice and a jug of water were thrust into the cell. A terse instruction delivered in Chinese was translated for Mont by Han. "We are wanted. We must be ready soon."

"Wanted for what?" Mont asked.

"Fujing Toy is master of Sum Yop Tong. Chinese war lord. When he meet other Tongs, he must impress them with his power and wealth."

"Meaning you and me go on display?"

"Yes," Han agreed. "If other Tong lords see plenty wealth, then maybe they settle fight with talk-talk."

The giant took his bowl of rice. The cup disappeared within his massive hand. One swallow and all the rice disappeared.

"Is that all they feeds you?" Mont asked.

"Fujing Toy keep me weak so I cannot escape."

Mont looked at his own bowl of rice, then at the huge man. "Whyn't you take this away from me?"

"No," Han replied, "we are brother prisoners. It not right."

Mont picked up Han's empty bowl. After a moment's thought, he scooped half of his rice into it and handed it to Han.

"Why you do?" the man asked.

"I'm smaller than half of you," Mont replied. "Reckon you need a lot more'n me."

At the far end of the reception hall, Mont could see Han standing stiffly at attention beside the door. Han's arms folded across his chest were at the height of the other men's heads, while his head was on a level with the lanterns hanging from the ceiling. He was dressed in finely embroidered silk to match the wall hangings, and he might have been mistaken for a carved pillar or over-sized statue.

Mont's own place was beside Fujing Toy's throne. Mont was wearing a long coat that hung below his knees and a pair of pointed-toed slippers. Around his head a cloth was wound, and then a long cane pole topped with a fan of peacock tail feathers was placed in his hand. He was instructed to wave the fan gently toward Fujing Toy, but under no circumstances to move from his place unless told to do so.

An audience was in progress. Several Chinese merchants had come to complain that boo-how-doys from rival Tongs had vandalized their businesses and injured their employees. Mont gathered this from watching the gestures and exclamations of the merchants, and from seeing the bandaged clerks holding broken merchandise. That the subjects were impressed with the wealth of Fujing Toy's palace was also apparent from the expressions on their faces.

More than once the Tong lord had gestured toward Mont as part of the furniture and fixtures, but the merchants were even more impressed with Han. With his long face, high cheekbones exaggerated by the hollows beneath them, and his implacable features, Han looked to Mont like a Chinese angel of death.

More important from Mont's point of view was the fact that Han drew all the attention to the opposite end of the room. The little boy was then able to pick up pieces of dried fish from a serving cart and fill his pockets. Later, Mont saved one small piece for himself and gave the rest to Han.

Tom's first glimpses of Virginia City were not

inspiring, to say the least. After the awesome scenery of the High Sierras and the majesty of Lake Tahoe, the descent to Carson and the barren hills of the Washoe Valley reminded Tom of the Hebrews turning back to the desert after glimpsing the Promised Land.

Clouds of acrid dust churned up from the wheels of the Pioneer Line coach as if a perpetual sandstorm accompanied the stage. The fine gray powder settled on everything. *In everything,* Tom thought as he futilely tried to clean out his grit-caked eyes and ears.

Glancing at the other passengers with their sour expressions and comical appearances, Tom imagined ruefully how silly he must look. Shirts became a uniform shade of dun, as did beards, hats, hair, boots, coats and trousers. The only exceptions made matters worse: where weary travelers wiped their faces, a lighter shade of grayish-pink contrasted with the surrounding darkness till everyone resembled either piebald horses or war-painted Indians.

The coach rattled onto C Street past brick buildings, timbered sheds, and canvas awnings. The principal decorations seemed to be handbills. Silently acknowledging the barrenness of the surroundings, the advertisements covered every available wall, post, and boulder. Each strove to outdo the others with bright colors, flamboyant claims, and lurid drawings. *Buy Dr. Fry's Liver Tonic,* shouted one. It posed a consumptive, bald man with a sunken chest next to a robust fellow with a full head of hair. Another ordered, *Look Here! Square Meals at the Howling Wilderness Saloon!*

Mounds of pale dirt and dark ore were piled around

every curve and beside each level stretch of road. The dumps from the mines formed conical heaps like the frenzied work of giant, demented ants.

Over the entire scene hung a pall of white steam compounded with black smoke and mixed liberally with noise. An incessant battering from the hundreds of stamps in the mills crushed quartz rock into rubble, and rubble into gravel, and gravel into sand, with a pounding as if the mountain's heart beat just beneath the surface.

The stagecoach pulled up in front of the Pioneer Company office. Near at hand was a bar called the Fancy Free and a billiard parlor of doubtful reputation known as the Boys' Retreat. Nearby was the Tahoe Hotel and the much advertised Howling Wilderness Saloon.

The storm of dirt that accompanied the travelers roiled up and over the coach, and for a time Virginia City disappeared behind a curtain of dust. All nine passengers inside the coach gave way to fits of coughing. Eyes streaming tears, Tom stumbled out of the stage, vaguely wondering if the six passengers riding on top had fared better or worse than he.

When the air cleared to the point of being breathable, the buildings of C Street reappeared. Tom retrieved his carpetbag and crossed the busy road toward the Tahoe Hotel. The ground underfoot was formed of a curious pavement-mixture known as "mining camp macadam": dirt, broken boards, cast off boots, battered tin cups and ragged playing cards, all stuck together with tobacco juice.

"Tom! Tom Dawson!"

The familiar, friendly sounding voice with the funny

drawling whine at the end of the words floated over the passing rumble of an eight-ox team hauling a high-sided ore wagon.

Oh no! thought Tom. *Someone who knows me has spotted me. This is sure to give me away.* He scanned the streets, sidewalks and storefronts, but could not locate the source of the greeting till the voice called out again, "Hey, Tom, up here!"

Behind him and on the balcony of the Stage Company office was Sam Clemens. Sam and Tom had known each other in Missouri, and both had left about the same time with similar desires to get away from that war-torn area. Sam was . . . a writer and something in politics. Tom had gotten a letter. He could not remember exactly what, only that Sam's brother, Orion, had been an official of the territory and had planned to get Sam a post.

"Hey, Sam," Tom waved. "Good to see you!"

"Stay right there," Clemens ordered. "I'm coming down."

In a few seconds the skinny young man with the wavy dark-brown hair and the drooping moustache appeared in the street beside Tom. His black frock coat, plaid vest and baggy trousers spoke of money and quality, but were wrinkled and creased. *Sam always did have a rumpled look,* Tom thought.

Sam grasped Tom's hand and pumped it vigorously in genuine pleasure at the reunion. "It is so good to see you," he drawled. "Now things can get lively again around here." As he spoke, a pair of brawling miners crashed through the doors of the Fancy Free Saloon and wound up wrestling in the dust twenty feet from where the two friends stood. No one in Virginia City, least of all Sam Clemens, paid any attention.

"Where you staying? International Hotel, of course," Sam both asked and answered.

"No," corrected Tom. "The Tahoe."

"That dump?" questioned Clemens. "No, no. It'll burn down most any day. Why, the way the wind blows right through its walls, the management has taken to advertising 'scenic views' from the mountains of sand that pile up in the corners!"

"Come with me, Sam," suggested Tom. "I promise I'll explain, if you'll just wait till we're in the room and don't question anything you hear me say."

Clemens narrowed his bushy brows and his eyes twinkled with mischievous delight. "I love mysteries," he said. "We haven't had a mystery in Virginia since some unknown scoundrel substituted a woodcut of a skunk for the profile of the publisher on the masthead of—"

Tom never got to hear the conclusion of that story, because right then a runaway horse and buckboard came plunging and careening down C Street directly toward the two men. The snorting and bucking chestnut draft animal was racing as if his life depended on getting away from the wagon chasing him.

Tom grabbed Sam and threw both of them aside and to the ground, rolling under the belly of a parked ore wagon. There was a terrific crash as the runaway horse pivoted away at the last second, spilling the buckboard broadside into the ore wagon. The buckboard's rear axle broke with the force of the impact, sending a spinning wheel flying under the ore wagon. It narrowly missed

Tom's head, bounced off the boardwalk and rebounded to land on top of the two friends.

Clemens opened one eye and peered around cautiously. "I think it's done," he said in a shaky sort of voice. As they crawled out from under the ore wagon and dusted each other off, he regained his sense of humor and added, "Greetings from the Comstock! That's what I call a real Washoe welcome—almost crushed and decapitated at the same time—show me another town that can arrange that!"

The buckboard's owner, a short Irishman with flame-red hair came running up. "For the love of . . . What could uv did it? I had me rig's brake set."

"Ah," demanded Clemens sternly, "but did you have the horse's brake set as well?"

Nighttime at the Tahoe Hotel. The shabby, makeshift furniture and the thin, bare walls and floor contrasted hugely with the remembered beauty of the hotel's name-sake. Tom prepared for bed by hanging his clothes over the foot of the cobbled-together bed frame and his hat on the nail that protruded from the door. He placed the Colt Navy near at hand on the wobbly table that served as nightstand, desk, and makeshift dresser, and blew out the oil lamp.

When he lay down on the straw-stuffed mattress, more grayish dust puffed upward. As tired as he was, Tom did not expect to get to sleep soon. Even if the hurdy-gurdy music from downstairs had not come up in full volume through the floor, the hammered piano tunes from the saloon next door or the jangling banjo from the dance hall across the street would have served to keep him conscious.

Taking stock of his situation, Tom was not impressed with his prospects of accomplishing anything useful on the Comstock. As he had explained to Sam that afternoon, he did not know who was to contact him, did not know what he would be asked to do, and in any case, did not have Mont with him to identify a supposed conspirator as part of any real threat.

Clemens had agreed. "There's fifteen—maybe twenty—thousand folks living on the lead between Virginia, Gold Hill and Silver City—more if you include every canyon round about. Every one of them is crazy all right—but about speculating in silver, not about the war."

Ownership of the Comstock mines was by the *foot,* measured along the lead. Stock in the Ophir mine was being sold at over two thousand dollars per foot; that of the Gould and Curry at just under four thousand. These proven producers were mining such rich ore that any rock assayed at less than fifty dollars of silver per ton was discarded as being not worth the trouble.

But according to Sam, the speculation was wildly inflated and dangerously fraudulent: "No more than twenty out of hundreds of mines have ever paid expenses, let alone showed a profit, but that doesn't stop the speculators, no sir. Let a man turn one shovelful of dirt and pretty soon he's printed fancy stock certificates and listed on the Frisco Change as a 'promising prospect.' Next he buys new clothes, a fancy rig and dinners for his friends, and pays for it all with *feet!* And *everybody* accepts it!"

The fantasy outstripped the reality, but even so, Sam reported that the mines were producing and shipping close to a *ton* of bullion a *day*. That information would be attractive to anyone outside the law, whether rebel operative or common thief.

The loud music from downstairs took on a frantic tone as the accompanying din of loud voices swelled to include the sounds of smashing furniture and shattering glass. That a brawl was breaking out was neither a surprise to Tom nor did it interest him.

He got out of bed and stood at the window in his night shirt. His mind was far from the Comstock mines, the rebels, and the war. He stared out his south-facing window and cast his thoughts across the intervening three hundred or so miles between Virginia City and Greenville . . . and Emily.

He missed her—missed having her to talk to—missed her gentle, forthright counsel. Too bland, that thought— he missed her warm smile and the way she lit up a room: he thought about her honey-blonde hair and the way she looked dressed in blue calico. The vagrant image of Belle Boyd entered his mind—saucy curls, white throat and exotic perfume. Tom shook his head as if to banish the distraction: he wanted to think about Emily and nothing else.

Trying to return to thoughts of Emily was not possible, even when the ghost of Belle had vanished into the dusty Comstock air. A volley of gunshots broke out downstairs as the ruckus escalated one more notch. A musical crash came as a hurdy-gurdy player dove for cover. The sounds of many booted feet running toward the exits added to the impression of a stampede or a cavalry charge. More shots were fired and there was the sound of smashing glass as someone jumped through a window.

Tom was still facing the street when three loud rapping sounds spun him around. He could not see, but he could smell a new cloud of dust floating about the room. Edging around the wall to the nightstand, Tom relit the oil lamp.

The blanket that covered the straw-filled mattress had three new holes in it that Tom did not recall. Grasping the corner of the bed frame and giving a downward yank that flipped it toward him, Tom pulled it over on its side. Sure enough, in the planks of the wooden floor, grouped directly beneath the center of where the bed had stood, were three bullet holes. A hand's breadth would have covered the spread.

CHAPTER 14

"Han," Mont asked after they were locked in for the night. "You could be the greatest warrior Fujing has. Why don't you join his boo-how-doys for real? Then they'd feed you real good and not keep you in this cage."

The giant looked distressed that Mont would suggest such a thing. "Oh no," he said. "They are bad men who kill with guns and hatchets. If I join, then this is what I will have to do also . . . and for what? So Fujing Toy can rule over three more streets of frightened shopkeepers? It is better this way."

"But if you was free, couldn't you defend them shop-keepers? Help 'em out?"

Han seemed thoughtful. "Back in my mountain home, this is what a man once said to me. He told me that God wanted me to use my great size to help others. When I asked him which god wanted this, he named one I did not know—Christos."

Clapping his hands in surprise and delight, Mont exclaimed, "He meant Jesus Christ. Han, that man was a Christian."

The giant agreed. "So, I found out later. But I was taken away as a slave and heard him speak no more. Perhaps you can tell me about him, the one called strong and gentle?"

" 'Deed I can," said Mont. " 'Deed I can!"

The small amount of sleep Tom caught the rest of that night came while sitting cross-legged on the floor and leaning back in a corner of the room. Just before dawn there was a furtive tap at the door, then the lockless knob turned, and the panel was pushed inward.

Tom made no sound. He slowly elevated the muzzle of the Colt until a .36 caliber slug was ready to greet an unwanted visitor. The door continued to swing open, but no one came in. From the shadows of the hallway, Tom heard a muttered exclamation and then the whispered comment, "Something's wrong. He's not in there!"

Two vaguely seen forms advanced into the room. When both were clearly inside the doorway and their dark shapes plainly outlined against the paler walls, Tom cocked the Navy. The double ratchet and locking click had an air of authority in the tiny room. Both figures stopped dead still, one with a foot upraised in mid-step.

At last a nervous voice spoke. "Mister, whoever you are . . . we are not armed."

"*I am,*" commented Tom, "and if you don't want further proof, you'd better walk to the far end of the room and lean your palms up against the wall." The two men complied.

Rising from the floor at last, Tom struck a match against the thumbnail of his left hand and touched it to the lamp's wick. Eyes and gun barrel never left their target.

By the warm glow of the oil lamp, Tom could see that the two were well dressed. Both men were shorter than he, one with light brown, wavy hair, the other with slicked back, dark hair. "Turn around slow," he ordered, "and keep your hands out where I can see them."

"Are you Wilson?" asked the dark-haired one when he had turned.

Tom offered no confirmation and only waited to see what would follow. The lighter-haired man, younger than the other, slowly lowered his hands.

"If you are Wilson," he said, "then there is no need for that gun. I am Hastings and this is Ingram. The word is Chapman."

"Why so nervous, Wilson?" asked the one referred to as Ingram. "Are you always this cautious, or have you been followed?"

"I generally get like this when somebody tries to plug me when I'm sleeping." Tom gestured with the gun barrel toward the overturned bed. "See for yourselves."

Hastings looked at the splintered trio of bullet holes and gave a low whistle. "Who is trying to kill you?" he asked.

"I thought you fellas might be able to answer that question," Tom replied. "Where were the two of you last night?"

"Listen, Wilson," said Ingram, "if that's really your name. Accidental shootings are five for a quarter around this town. Sure, you got cause to be upset, but coming up through the floor like that . . . if someone had meant to kill you, he did a mighty poor job of it."

Tom frowned at the thought that maybe it had been a mindless act by some drunk after all. He lowered the hammer of the Colt to the half-cock safety.

Ingram continued in a less belligerent tone. "Besides, if Hastings or me *had* fired those shots, would we come around here this morning? 'Howdy do, Mr. Innkeeper. Find any fresh corpses this morning? Mind if we lay claim to one?' "

"Why *are* you here before sunup?" Tom asked.

Ingram refused to answer any questions. He said Tom had to prove his identity as a member of the conspiracy. After being satisfied that Tom had been sent by Jasper Perry, he explained the early morning visit. "We don't think we should be seen in public together. Hastings and I even came here by different routes. Too much depends on pulling this off for us to take a tumble now."

"What is the delay?" Tom asked. "Perry seemed to think you'd have the money by now."

Ingram looked angry as Hastings answered in a chagrinned tone. "It's the boom . . . bonanza . . . flush times. Call it what you will, the Comstock is *too* successful. All the men we thought we could count on are either mining or speculating. All those traitorous souls who pledged an oath to our Glorious Cause have renounced their vows for the sake of silver. But to arm the *Chapman* and seize a steamer, we must act soon."

Tom turned the bed back upright and gestured for his visitors to be seated. Finally he was getting close to the plan. He did keep the Colt in his folded arms while he remained standing with his back to the corner. "So what's to be done? We three are not enough to take an Express wagon by force."

"Working on it," said Ingram gruffly. "We'll have help when the time comes. We've got one superintendent who may still honor his oath."

"And what do you want me to do?" Tom inquired.

"We need better information on shipments. Any way you could get close to a mine official or an assayer? Someone who might hear news of a useful nature?"

Tom appeared to be thinking for a time before he answered, even though his mind had jumped immediately to what he thought was a perfect strategy. "Well," he said slowly, "I do know a reporter for the *Enterprise*."

Sam was agreeable to participating in the ruse. "Sure, I can pretend to take you in, show you around, that sort of thing. But these fellas aren't too bright, else they'd know that nobody *ever* tells a reporter the truth!"

Tom grinned. "I didn't know you had made such a name for yourself, *Mark Twain*," he quipped, leaning heavily on the writer's pseudonym.

"A passing fancy," said Sam, airily waving an unlit Eureka cigar. "There's no fame and glory in writing satire. But what about your safety? And mine, I might add. What if these characters are dangerous, even if they aren't smart? Why not turn them in now?"

"I thought of that," Tom replied, "but there's still a bigger group out there, including this mine official, whoever he is. I don't want to alarm the rest if we can identify them all."

"All right, let's start poking around today, and day after tomorrow I'll take you down in a mine. I always get a good reception. Royal treatment. Just the fact that a reporter is looking raises the price of the 'feet' by a hundred dollars or so.

"By the way," he added, picking up his flat-crowned, rolled brim hat, "I wouldn't worry too much about the shots from below. Friend of mine was sitting on his bed taking off his boots. He was just straightening up when a celebratory bullet came up through the floor, right between his feet. Carried away an eyebrow and a lock of his hair."

"What did he do?" asked Tom.

"Same as you're fixing to do . . . changed hotels."

Mont was awakened by the noise of Han exercising. Uncurling himself from the single blanket and the pile of straw on which he lay, Mont opened one eye and peered around.

In a corner of the room was Han. His legs were braced against the floor and the upper half of his body strained against the brick wall as if he were trying to push it over. *Like Samson,* Mont thought.

Mont waited until the exercise was complete, then asked in a low voice, "Han, why didn't you try to escape again before you lost your strength?"

Regarding Mont as if deciding whether to tell him or not, Han at last said, "If Han escape once more, Fujing say boo-how-doy put out my eyes."

"But you can't live like this," Mont said angrily. "They can't keep you between starvin' and blind."

"Ah, my little friend, but they can," Han said.

" 'Pears to me," Mont concluded, "what we really need is a permanent escape."

The next day was Sunday, but from the window of the International Hotel where Tom now had a room, the tramp of men toward the seven o'clock shift changes looked like any other morning. Four dollars a day was the going wage for a hard-rock mine. A man could take Sunday off if he elected to, but, of course, he went unpaid.

Giving up one seventh of your income was more than most would do. Living on the Comstock was not cheap. With two-dollar rooms and fifty-cent meals, four dollars did not stretch very far—not far enough to cover a whole day lost.

Tom turned around at a knock on his door, laying his hand on the Colt. He relaxed when he heard Sam's cheery greeting, and Clemens entered the room. "Watching the parade of honest miners?" he asked.

A steady stream of denim-clad men flowed past. Almost to a man, each was bearded, hatted, and booted. Then Tom noticed one figure that stood out. He did wear denim and boots, but his white hair was uncovered and the face clean-shaven. What was more, the man seemed too frail and stoop-shouldered to be a miner.

"Who's that?" Tom asked, pointing.

"That's my good friend, the Reverend Bollin, on his way to conduct services," Sam replied. "Looks like a broken-down prospector from the days of '49, doesn't he? But he's a lot tougher than he looks. Been here since the beginning practically."

"Where does he preach?"

Sam's eyes twinkled as he said, "Right in the teeth of Satan . . . a little district called Devil's Gate. Has a regular church there, too. When he holds forth with one of his two-fisted, sin-killing, devil-chasing sermons, the monte dealers head for the city limits. He gets up early to catch the men coming off shift, and he'll preach three times today."

"Is he as old as he looks?"

"Older, maybe. His son David is running a mission church in Hawaii that the father founded back in the '20s."

"Can I meet him? He sounds like someone who knows what's happening around here."

"Sure," agreed Sam, surprised at the sudden interest in the preacher. "I'll fix it for tonight."

Just as Tom and the good reverend had settled down in the parson's cottage for a cup of coffee, there was the sound of running feet and urgent pounding on the door.

Pastor Bollin opened it to find a raggedly dressed boy of ten or eleven years bent over on the front step, trying to catch his breath. "What is it, son? What's wrong?"

The boy fluttered a hand across his chest to signal his

inability to talk. The pastor called for Tom to bring a glass of water while he patted the child's heaving back. Presently, the spasmodic shuddering of the boy's shoulders eased and the single-knotted suspender holding up his overalls stopped bunching up and down.

"Come . . . quick," the child gasped, "Miss Eva . . . hurt bad . . . Miss Sally sent me."

"I'll just be a moment," said the pastor. "Let me get my coat." He emerged with a coat and Bible. To Tom he apologized, "I'm sorry. We can have our visit another time."

"No apology needed, Pastor. Mind if I come with you? Maybe I can be of help."

The preacher sized up Tom's six-foot-plus frame and remarked, "Maybe you can at that. The house where Miss Eva lives is below D street. It can be a very rough area."

The hike from the pastor's home on the hillside above A Street went straight down the incredibly steep slope to which Virginia City clung. On the way, the small messenger gasped out his story.

"Miss Eva has a steady caller name of Stone. He a powerful mean secesh. Tonight he catch her with a Yankee feller. The men, they go to tusslin' and Miss Eva, she try to stop 'em."

"Yes, boy, and what happened?"

The boy gulped as if even retelling the next part frightened him. "Miss Eva, she got stabbed! The Yankee, he run off. Miss Sally hear the screamin' and try to help, but Stone won't even let her in. He drunk and he says Miss Eva got what's comin' to her. Miss Sally send me for you."

The row of shabby clapboard one-room houses that formed the Maiden Lane of Virginia City soon came into sight. In front of one stood a woman screaming at a man who fended her off by waving a Bowie knife in her face. His other hand held a large pistol.

"All right, son," said the pastor, "I understand now. You run along home."

Tom drew his Colt and checked the loads, but Pastor Bollin laid a cautionary hand on his arm. "Let's see what we can do without more bloodshed first," he said. "Stone is a genuine killer who will shoot us both and, no doubt, some other innocent bystanders, if we crowd him."

Tom replaced the weapon in its holster and dropped a few paces behind the preacher. Bollin went directly up to the hysterical woman and drew her back from the doorway. "Keep her away," slurred Stone. "Else I'll give her some of what the other tramp got! Serve her right," he muttered, "taking up with Yankees."

"Help her, preacher," sobbed the woman. "She's dying in there. . . . I heard her scream! Won't somebody *do* something?"

Pastor Bollin passed the woman to Tom, asking him to stay by her, then he confronted Stone from two arms length away. "Lijah," he said, "it's not like you to pick on women. Let me see to Miss Eva. Quickly, man!"

"No!" thundered the cutthroat. "I ain't never put no woman in my private cemetery a'fore this, but this'n deserves it! Ain't no business for a Bible-thumper, any road."

"You aren't thinking straight, Stone," argued Pastor Bollin. "This town won't stand for it. There'll be a posse after you with a rope if she dies. For your own good, then, let me help her." As if adding her agreement, an anguished groan came from the wounded woman inside the house.

It was more than Sally could stand. She squirmed in Tom's grasp on her shoulders, twisting to reach the Colt Navy. "I won't let her die!" she yelled, drawing the pistol and wrestling with Tom.

Stone saw the struggle and raised his own pistol. Before he could aim, the preacher had stepped inside his guard and knocked the gun hand aside. Stone's pistol discharged into the ground with an explosion that caused the growing crowd of curious onlookers to dive for cover. He gave a bellow like an angry bull and aimed a knife-thrust at the preacher's chest.

Pastor Bollin parried the jab with his large black leather-bound Bible. The sharp tooth of the Bowie penetrated cover and pages, but was caught and swept aside. Bollin followed this move with an overhand right that arced down on Stone's eye with a crunch that drove him to his knees. Without even waiting for any further outcome, the preacher jumped past the outlaw and crashed open the door.

Stone started to rise. His pistol was aimed at the preacher's back, and he was thumbing back the hammer when Tom leapt on him from behind. The gun flew from his grasp and slid into the house. It came to rest beside Pastor Bollin where he knelt next to a woman lying on the floor in a pool of blood.

Tom and Lijah Stone rolled over and over on the muddy slope of Virginia City. Tom was the stronger of the two, but he held off the knife with difficulty since the outlaw outweighed him by forty pounds.

A savage chop downward thrust the Bowie into the hillside, just missing Tom's left ear. As he concentrated on keeping the knife-hand tied up, Stone unleashed a roundhouse left that hit Tom over the other ear.

Tom threw his weight into pulling around on Stone's captive right arm. As they rolled over yet again, Tom thrust his forearm up across Stone's throat as hard as he could. The larger man's eyes bulged and the knife flipped from his fingers as they clawed at the earth. Tom threw the forearm yet again, his elbow this time smashing into the side of Stone's head. The big man sagged, gasping for air.

Tom retrieved the Bowie and thrust it into his own belt, then entered the cabin. Pastor Bollin was tearing a bed sheet into bandages and using them to bind up Eva's wounds. At his side was a softly crying Sally who kept repeating, "Will she live? Will she live?"

Completing his work before he responded, the preacher at last replied, "You must pray now. We have done all that can be done till Doc Warner arrives. The knife wounds on her face and arms aren't deep. The worst one, the one in her chest, turned on a rib and is not as bad as I feared. But she has lost a lot of blood and won't be out of danger for some time."

Tom picked up Pastor Bollin's Bible. A jagged tear penetrated over halfway through, but stopped with the tip resting on Psalm 91. "Thy truth will be my shield" the verse read.

CHAPTER 15

Tom was pulling a pair of canvas overalls on over his Levis and flannel shirt. The borrowed work outfit was discolored with brown dirt and streaked with the traces of black and yellow ores. It was sweat-stained, and the shoulders were spotted with drops of candle wax.

He paused before adding the floppy felt hat with the dented crown that completed the mining costume. "If I'd come to Virginia City dressed like this," he said, laughing at Sam who was similarly 'fitted out,' "you'd never have recognized me."

Sam nodded his agreement but added, "That's because you stood out like the thirty-five foot flag waving on top of Sun Mountain. Now you look like one of the boys."

Sam took his turn to laugh at Tom's grimace before he continued, "You know, the boys figger you for real brave, standing up to Lijah Stone like that."

"Oh?" Tom replied blandly. "You can't call it bravery if there isn't any choice. I'd say the real courage was shown by Pastor Bollin."

"No dispute there, but I hear tell that you had your hand in it, too. The boys think you should have killed Stone while you had the chance. How soon does your stage leave?"

"You know I'm not through here yet," Tom replied. "Do 'the boys' figger me to run away?"

Sam looked genuinely concerned for his friend. "You don't understand," he said seriously. "Lijah Stone chews railroad spikes for amusement, but that's not how he got those notches on his pistol grips. You shamed him and he'll be on the shoot for you till he cleans his reputation."

"Why isn't Stone arrested for attempted murder? Isn't there any law and order in this town?"

"Course there is, or at least there's plenty of law—every third rock's got a lawyer under it. But 'order'—now, that's altogether different. Judge Turner swore out a warrant for Stone's arrest, but he can't get anybody to serve it!"

Tom snorted with disgust. "That's enough about the quaint customs in Washoe," he said. "Let's go look at a mine."

The two friends fell in with a file of miners walking toward the shafts of the Gould and Curry Mine. "There are three ways into the diggings," Sam instructed. "We can walk in through a long tunnel in the side of the hill, we can climb down a thousand feet of ladders, or we can ride the lift. What'll you have?"

"Seems to me the lift would be the easiest," Tom observed. "Let's go that route."

"Everybody says that," replied Sam with a grin. "Just remember, I *did* give you a choice."

The hoist operator greeted Sam like an old friend. When Tom was introduced, the man respectfully removed his hat and shook his hand with reverence. Tom was puzzled until the man glanced around, then announced, "It's about time someone stood up to Stone. Nice to have you visit us. When you're ready to come up, give me three rings, then three more."

The lift platform was only four feet square and made of oak planks, reminding Tom of the door to the hay loft back home. The lift was suspended from the four corners and the center by ropes that met in an iron ring hanging from a cable ten feet over their heads.

Both men stepped onto the platform and reached for the center rope. "You may want to use both hands," Sam observed when Tom grasped it with only one.

"Why?" Tom started to ask, "How fast does this thing . . . ?" when suddenly the tiny section of wooden floor dropped toward the center of the earth!

"How . . . does . . . it . . . stop?" shouted Tom as the square patch of daylight dwindled overhead and the lift shot into the mountain's heart.

"Clutches," the reply was bellowed back. "If the operator doesn't misjudge or the cables snap!"

"What happens then?" Tom's words whirled up the shaft.

Tom thought he heard the words "An inquest," and just then the platform slowed and the stretching and contracting cables bounced the lift to a halt.

At the top of the shaft, the lift operator hummed contentedly to himself. He was pleased to have shaken the hand of the man who bested Lijah Stone in a fight. *"Do you remember sweet Betsy from Pike?"* he sang in an off-key tenor.

From behind a pile of cable spools stepped a man whose battered face bore the marks of a recent battle. The butt of the Colt in his hand had a string of notches filed into it. He stepped almost casually up to the lift operator and stuck the barrel of the Colt in the man's ear.

"What the . . . ?" the operator stammered, then stopped abruptly and his eyes grew wide with fear.

The hoarse, rasping voice of Lijah Stone demanded,

"Was you sayin' you were glad someone stood up to me, Clay? How was that again?"

The operator stuttered, "Mister Stone . . . I didn't mean . . . that is, you . . ."

The gun's muzzle twisted into Clay's ear. "Now suppose you just shut your mouth and listen so's I don't have to clean your ears with this here forty-four. You know, I always wanted to know how to run a hoise, and you're gonna show me."

Pushing aside two swinging half doors, Sam and Tom stepped into a rock-walled chamber that opened to a tunnel running across in front of them. Miners, all dressed exactly as Tom, passed in front of them. Some were carrying picks or shovels and a few transported heavy-looking wooden crates marked "danger—explosives."

But the first thing that caught Tom's eyes was the timbering. Huge square posts, eighteen inches thick, supported a framework of similar shoring all across the ceiling. By the flickering oil lamps hanging at intervals along the tunnel, Tom could see the cells made of beams marching into the far distance.

"Deidesheimer square sets," Sam explained in response to Tom's look. "The hard-headed Dutchman wouldn't believe it when people said you couldn't mine this deep without cave-ins. Said he got his inspiration from looking at honeycombs. Whole forests of trees have been replanted down here."

"So this here lever runs the cage up and down, is that

it?" questioned Lijah Stone.

Clay, the lift operator, nodded slowly, grimacing at the feel of the gun barrel in his ear and the harsh grating of Stone's voice.

"And this little red knob speeds the whole shebang up or slows it down?"

Again, a single nervous nod.

"My, my," chuckled Stone hoarsely. "Ain't we learnin' fast?"

Stone removed the muzzle of the Colt from Clay's ear and negligently waved it around the little room that contained the hoist controls. "And when someone wants brought up or down, that there bell rings?" he asked, pointing with the Colt.

"Yes sir, Mr. Stone, it surely does."

"And the signals tells you what direction and how far, even who it is doin' the ringin'?"

"Yes sir," Clay agreed, trying to sound obliging. "It's kinda like a private telegraph, don'cha see and . . ." He stopped abruptly, afraid that he'd been too agreeable.

"So when the scribbler and his tin-horn friend want to get all the way back up here, it'll ring three times and then three more, and won't nobody else ring that ring. Well, well."

The two friends walked down one of the seemingly endless corridors. "Try not to think about the thousand feet of solid rock that these tiny tree stumps are holding over your head," Sam said with malicious glee. "Actually," he continued, "the biggest problem down here is water, not rock. You get . . . well, here, see for yourself."

At intervals along the gallery, drifts opened on either side, and in these men were working. As the vein of silver ore slanted downward into the great mountain, the ant-like efforts of humans followed.

The ringing of picks and the clatter of shovels echoed noisily out of the right-hand chamber. As Tom and Sam stepped to look, a yellow-bearded man with enormous shoulders pushed an ore car up out of the blackness along a narrow set of rails. "Step aside, please, gents," he said as he muscled past with a quarter ton of bluish-black rock. Tom pressed himself back against the tunnel wall to avoid being run over by the cart; only the thickness of the timber sets gave room to stand.

"Say, friend," Sam called to the miner, "are they pumping on this level?"

The miner shook his head, waving the candle mounted in the reflector on his hat. "Down one more," he said.

The rattle of tin lunch pails and the stomping of boots alerted Stone to the approach of a group of men. He stepped back behind the stack of cable spools. "Now, Clay," he advised the lift operator, "you just do your job nice and easy like. I like you, but this here Colt ain't so sure . . . and it has a nasty habit of blowin' big holes in things it don't like."

The group of miners tramped onto the lift platform and waved at Clay. "Goin' down to three," one of them hollered.

As Clay moved the lever and pulled the red knob, the great spool unwound and lowered the men into the shaft. If Clay acted any differently than usual, the miners never indicated any notice.

In the next chamber on the left, the ore had already been removed. All that remained in its place was a dark hole from which a ladder protruded. A rhythmic chugging noise came up from the hole. "How far down is it to the next level?" Tom asked.

Sam shrugged. "Hard to say. That little black hole may be twenty feet deep or may be eighty. Two days ago a miner slipped and fell in one like it. Dropped over a hundred feet. His funeral is today."

Tom was extra cautious in the placement of his feet on the rungs and his grip on the ladder as they descended. When they reached the bottom, they discovered a steam engine was the source of the chugging sound. It was struggling to operate a pump to drain a sulphury-smelling pool of steaming water.

The two men stood for a while in the stench and the noise, but exited to a quieter drift before speaking. "There you see the real difficulty facing the Comstock," Sam pointed out. "Sometimes just the swing of a pick will bust through a place and water will come pouring in faster than it can be pumped out."

"And hot, smelly water at that," Tom observed.

Sam nodded. "Scalding sometimes. More than one miner has died from burns. After the cave-in that hit the Ophir mine, one entire gallery flooded in the space of two hours."

"I thought you said the square-set timbering prevented cave-ins."

The light from the candle flickered on the merriment in

Sam's eyes and his teasing grin. "I did not say 'eliminated.'"

"What would happen if you was drunk on the job?" asked Stone. "Couldn't you drop some folks clean to the bottom and squash 'em like eggs?"

"No," maintained Clay stoutly. "This rig has got a governor and a . . ." The sound of what he was about to say rattled through his head, mimicking the chatter of his teeth.

"A what?" Stone demanded.

"A dead man set," Clay finished with a gulp. "It keeps the hoist from runnin' too fast or past the bottom gallery, or from flyin' out of the shaft comin' up."

"Hmm," Stone pondered out loud. "Then the only thing can go wrong real bad like is if that cable or them ropes should bust."

"So what is the answer to the problem with the flooding?" Tom asked as he and Sam returned to the hoist.

Sam shook his head. Little drops of candle wax ran off the sides of the candle holder and dripped from the brim of the felt hat onto the shoulders of his coveralls. "I don't know for certain. A man named Sutro claims he can tunnel clear up from the valley and hit the two thousand foot level here; drain the whole mountain."

"Do you think it'll work?"

"Some experts say it will. Others say it'll cost too blame much. It's eight miles down to the outlet from here. That's millions of dollars spent before one pound of ore much below where we're standing ever gets mined. Well, what do you think? Have you seen enough?"

At Tom's nod of agreement, Sam flicked the switch of the telegraph three times, a short pause, then three more.

Stone's face lit up with a broad smile that showed his missing front teeth when he heard the signal bell. He held his breath, and when it rang three more times, said exultantly to Clay, "Go on, Clay, send it to 'em. Don't be makin' 'em wait, now."

The lift dropped away empty into the blackness. Stone watched the great spool of cable unwind and lower downward till it slowed and finally stopped.

Over Clay's shoulder he asked, "How do you know when they're ready to come up?" Without Clay needing to reply, the signal bell gave one long continuous peal. "That's just fine," he remarked casually. Without warning he slammed the gun barrel into the side of Clay's head, and as the operator slumped to the floor, Stone yanked back on the lever.

"The boys say the Comstock is the richest silver lode in the world," Sam commented as the lift started up the shaft.

"What exactly does that mean?" Tom asked. The hoist pulled even with another gallery, then continued upward between barren rock walls. The momentary glimpse of miners' candles looked like fireflies darting about in the cavern's gloom.

"It means that Virginia City and the other mining towns of the Comstock will ship somewhere between twenty and thirty *million* dollars of bullion *this year*."

The hoist was accelerating now, speeding upward past three galleries in quick succession. A brief swirl of cooler air blew on the two men as the mouth of each tunnel yawned and closed. "That makes this territory a real prize for . . . say, are we stopping?"

The platform slowed and halted with a jerking, bouncing motion and hung suspended. "Maybe somebody else is ready to . . . no, that can't be; we're between galleries." It was true: the flickering glow cast by the candlestubs burning in their hat-top holders showed four rough walls of granite with streaks of shiny quartz, but no opening.

"Confound that Clay," spouted Sam. "What's he playing at, anyway?"

At that moment, the platform started upward again with a bump. Sam just had time to remark "about time," when the cage stopped, then dropped suddenly. Beneath the candle's feeble light, Tom could see Sam's bushy eyebrows knit together in consternation.

"I bet that scoundrel Higbie is behind this," he said. "I wonder how much he paid Clay to give us a rough ride."

This descent did not end with a gently rocking bump. Instead, the cable stretched downward with a complaining creak. The lift rebounded sharply, as if someone had shifted from downward to upward without slowing the machinery.

Up charged the platform, gaining speed. Just as abruptly the hoist paused once more. The oak floor continued on a few feet by its own momentum, floating up the shaft before falling freely.

Before it could hit bottom, the winch was unwinding again, speeding the descending lift downward. Overhead the ropes securing the platform to the iron ring began to sing with an ominous twang and the platform yo-yoed up and down.

"Sam!" Tom called sharply as the hoist topped out another rapid ascent and again fell freely before hitting the end of the restraining cable. "Sam, this is no joke! Someone's trying to bust the platform loose!"

"What'll we do?" shouted Sam over the creaking, grinding sounds.

"Get ready to jump for the next tunnel mouth as we pass."

The next upward swoosh and downward plunge extinguished both candles. Now in pitch blackness, suspended hundreds of feet above a crushing impact, neither man could even see the other, much less the momentary shadow that meant a lead to safety. Far overhead, a tiny scrap of daylight winked mockingly.

"Now what?" Sam yelled.

"We'll have to jump one at a time. On the next drop, I'll drag my boot along the shaft," ordered Tom. "When I yell, jump!"

Sam tried to position himself to make the leap for his life. When the next stomach-wrenching swoop occurred, the hobnails of Tom's bootsole cast tiny sparks as the heads grated on the wall. Feeling the gap, Tom screamed.

With a fragment of a cry, Sam disappeared! One second he was on the platform and the next he flung himself outward through space. Tom was alone on the lift.

The platform hit the bottom of its fall. With the twangs

of bowstrings and the sharp cracks of pistol shots, two of the suspending ropes parted. The lift tipped toward the unsupported edge and began to drag along the rock walls, canted at a crazy angle. Tom clung desperately to the center support. His feet dangled over a gaping crack that would either drop him to oblivion, or catch him and crush him against the granite shaft.

Like a giant hand trying to shake off an obstinate drip of water, the platform rose and fell, almost jerking Tom's grip loose from the cord. His boots drummed a running clatter on the oak planks as he struggled to push back upward.

The lift rose and halted, then dropped again, slapping at Tom as if the platform were a threatening palm trying to swat him like a fly. He heard a shout from the blackness, "Tom!" it shouted. "Up here!"

Sam's voice, just above his head. Only one second to decide, an instant to make a choice which might be no choice at all, but a farewell.

Tom jumped for the unseen lip of the tunnel mouth; pushed off hard with his feet. One boot tangled in the center rope and spun him half around. His leap was not clean and only one hand caught the ledge of the passage. The other hand scrabbled for purchase, only to scrape bare rock.

His right arm and shoulder screamed with the pain of his weight hanging from his clawed hand. He heard the motion of the lift reverse and knew it would knock loose his fragile handhold, dropping him into the pit.

A dangling rope brushed his face—one of the broken support cables dragged over his shoulder. Another fraction of an instant to decide, then his wildly flailing left hand grabbed the rope. His body instantly jerked upward.

The handhold gone, Tom swung wildly, blindly, toward the tunnel mouth. He felt the rush of the lift at his feet when something wrapped around his knees, pulling him toward the darkness.

"I've got you," Sam yelled, and the two tumbled down together onto the rocky floor of the mine tunnel.

CHAPTER 16

The place Ingram selected was near the top of a grade on the climb out of the Tahoe Basin. Cedars and tall Ponderosa Pines surrounded the looping roadway so that only tiny glimpses of sky could be seen through the overhanging trees.

Snow had collected to a depth of eight feet all along this stretch of highway. Avery had heard the Pioneer Stage Company driver talk about the years before the drought when the snow had reached twenty or thirty-foot depths along the same route. He could scarcely credit such a story; believed it to be a whopper, until Ingram confirmed it as fact.

In years like those, the stage and express companies suspended their operations for the duration of the first big storm. Then they brought out special coaches built on sled runners that were able to glide over the icy surface. But this year and last, it had not been necessary. Several teams of mules drawing iron-bladed buck scrapers were kept in constant employment keeping the roadway clear.

The coaches operated in an eight-foot-deep canyon of

hard packed snow, but their wheels stayed in well-worn ruts, and commerce over the Sierras continued unchecked. The cleared passageway was just barely wide enough for two teams to pass each other, and heaven help the teamster who swung too wide on a blind curve.

Two hundred yards below the summit, the road made a sharp turn to the left coming out of a canyon. Next, a sharp switchback to the right for fifty yards elevated the coach almost to the peak, when another abrupt turn to the left reversed the direction of travel once more. Given the steepness of the grade and the icy conditions, drivers favored breaking into a gallop as soon as they came out of the canyon. They were trying to keep the momentum up all the way to the peak.

The highway plunged down again immediately after reaching the summit. There was no more than a five-hundred-foot-long level spot at the top of the ridge.

The most logical place for a holdup was just after the third switchback, when the horses were laboring on the steepest stretch. Their energy would be spent on the galloping climb and the coach would be starting to slow.

The straining bodies of the six-up team rippled with the demands of the load and the mountain. The salty-acrid odor of their effort drifted back to the driver on the wagon box.

Floyd was a careful driver; careful of his teams, if not always so cautious with the comfort of the passengers. He knew better than to push the horses till they sweated, and he kept the pace one notch less than enough to lather them, knowing that the thirty-five-degree air of the eight-thousand-foot pass would kill a sweaty horse the same as a man.

Passengers with their complaints about the ride and the temperature in the coach had always rubbed Floyd the wrong way. After all, he was completely out in the open all the time, right? What business did a puny, thin-skinned fare-payer have of voicing anything other than gratitude?

Floyd was grateful that he no longer had to cope with the foibles of passengers. Since leaving the Pioneer Stage Company to take on the Wells, Fargo express wagons, Floyd was much happier. He was still driving a six-in-hand over the same magnificent Alpine scenery, but now there were no whining passengers to bother him.

Glancing over his shoulder at the shotgun-toting guard in the wagon bed, Floyd wondered if he had any complaints. The difference was, guards were employees and Floyd was their boss as long as the wheels rolled—he could tell them to stow it. Not that this one made any complaints, or any small talk either. He was huddled down inside a fleece-lined jacket as if trying to disappear completely. Ordinarily, there were two guards on the box, but one had not appeared at departure time. "Drunk, more'n likely," Floyd had remarked to the station agent.

The two outriders were within call, but the one ahead appeared and vanished with each curve of the road. Floyd had not seen the one behind since they began the ascent of the Truckee.

The heavy iron ice shoes rang with every step up the grade, but the enforced slow pace made it a dismal sound, like the tolling of church bells for a funeral. Floyd noted the slack in the middle line of the three thick leather straps moving through the fingers of his left hand. He gave it a quick flip and called to the near-side bay of the swing team, "Get up there, Candy. Quit yer loafin'."

The guard in the box stirred and stretched, trying to ease the cramp of his leg muscles. Seeing the driver's glance, the man remarked, "It's almighty cold today, Floyd."

Letting rip a string of profanity, Floyd promised to make things real hot, real quick, if he had any more complaints. The nerve! All the guard had to do to earn his pay was sit tight and hold on to a twelve gauge. How would he like it if he had to sense every change of gait, every curve of the road, every different surface and—

A sudden shout from ahead brought Floyd out of his indignant reverie. He jerked his hand up and called to the guard, "Look sharp. May be trouble."

From around the bend of the road just ahead came Clive, the point rider. His hat was tied down over his ears with a bandanna or otherwise it would have flown off. He waved his arm and shouted, skidding his chestnut gelding to a stop beside the wagon.

"Floyd," Clive panted, "there's been an accident up ahead!"

"Bad one?"

"Powerful bad! Wagon turned over, two men down, blood all over!"

"Could you help any of 'em?"

Clive looked startled. "I come straight back here to tell you. I didn't think—"

"You sure enough didn't! Now get outta the way!"

Shaking the lines with a sudden snap, Floyd called to the leader, "Get up, Abel! Rattle your hocks, Ben!"

The express lurched into motion. "Fire a shot, Jerry," Floyd ordered the guard in the wagon bed. This was the signal for the drag rider to come up pronto. "And keep low. If this is some sort of trick, you be ready to go to blastin'."

The scene on the top of the rise was a grisly one, indeed. A Murphy wagon was upside down off the side of the road. One man was pinned beneath it. Only his floppy black hat covering his head and shoulders was visible. Another body lay flung like a rag doll on the snow on the other side of the road. Dark crimson blood streaked his face and clothes and was splashed on the snow bank all around.

Floyd stopped the express wagon as soon as the accident was in view. He gestured curtly to the guard, "Don't just sit there gawkin'! Get on up and see if you can help!"

Floyd regretted the missing guard. Talking aloud to himself he said, "You be watchin' the back-trail and the woods either side. Yup, that's the ticket."

Clive stepped off his horse, tying it to the wreck, and the box guard, Jerry, joined him beside the overturned wagon. Clive whistled a sharp note and shook his head. "There ain't nothin' to do for this one, Jerry. The box pert near cut him in two—musta throwed him off, then rolled acrost him."

Fingering the shotgun nervously and glancing around at the snow-covered trees, Jerry stayed far back. He was young and scared—Jerry was the Virginia City Station agent's nephew and he owed his job to that relationship.

Right at the moment, he was wishing he had stayed in Ohio; but his ma had sent him west to save him from the war, and here he was.

Clive crossed the icy expanse of roadway toward the blood-spattered second body. Jerking his attention away from the flattened figure, Jerry ran after the point rider.

In his haste to catch up, Jerry failed to account for his slick-soled boots and the skating-rink quality of the highway. Three running strides and he lost his balance, three awkwardly bouncing hops to try to regain it, and a backward sprawl in which both feet flew up in the air.

It cost him his pride and a sharp rap on the head, but it saved his life—at least for the moment. Clive was just bending over to examine the corpse when the body on the ground grinned through its mask of chicken blood and raised a sawn-off double-barrel from beneath a fold of oilcloth duster.

The load of double-shot at a distance of three feet almost cut Clive in half. Echoes of the shotgun's explosion bounced from rocky ledge to snow covered meadow and down the mountain slope, till the continuous roll sounded like thunder in the high peaks and clumps of snow fell from the trees.

Floyd saw the blast that killed Clive and whipped up his team. He drove with one hand, his calloused right fist closing around the double-barrelled scatter-gun he carried beside him and thumbing back the hammers.

"Keep down," he yelled to Jerry. The advice was unnecessary because the young guard had also seen Clive's death. Jerry crouched below the margin of snow bank that bordered the road. A second barrel of buckshot tore into the frozen crystals right in front of him, pelting him with icy fragments. He touched off a blast of his own shotgun without ever lifting his head from where he had it buried in the crook of his arm.

Behind him, the man under the faked wreck was having trouble struggling free. The set-up was almost too realistic, and for a moment he really was pinned. He fired two more shots at Jerry, but the depression of the roadbed coupled with his own prone position made the bullets pass harmlessly overhead.

The hooves of the six-up team clattered and skidded on the frozen lane. The express wagon lurched forward with Floyd standing upright on the driver's platform, holding his shotgun pressed tightly against his side. He fired a round at the robber who had just succeeded in crawling from beneath the wagon. The boom of the twelve gauge was like the climax of a conjuring trick: the bushwhacker dove head first back under the overturned wagon and disappeared.

Clive's horse reared against the reins by which it was tied to the tongue of the Murphy wagon. The second time the animal reared, plunging and kicking, the leather leads snapped and the horse bolted across the road.

Jerry heard the pounding hoofbeats, and in a move that would have done credit to an Oglala buffalo hunter, sprang up and grabbed the horse's neck. Using the animal's momentum to his own advantage, Jerry swung aboard the saddle. He discovered, to his amazement, that he still had the shotgun in his hands.

But the magic could not continue. Floyd could not reload as quickly as Clive's murderer could fling aside the sawed-off weapon and produce a Colt.

Three shots in quick succession hit Floyd high in the chest and toppled him from the wagon seat. He stood up tall as if to urge the team for one last burst of speed, then pitched headlong off the side.

The sudden yank to the left as Floyd fell, followed by the slack in the line, confused the six-up team. The leaders jerked the others off the road into deep snow. They continued to pull a short distance, floundering, then stopped.

Jerry saw Floyd shot off his perch, knew he was dead. Two shots from the Colt whipped past him, but he was already far enough away to spoil the aim. He never slackened his pace away from the scene, just rode as fast as he could for help.

Ingram wiped the chicken blood from his face on the sleeve of his duster and hurried over to the overturned wagon. "Get on out," he called sarcastically to Avery, who was still hiding under the wreck. "Fat lot of help you turned out to be. Whyn't you shoot?"

Trembling all over like an Aspen leaf in a high wind, Avery crawled out of his hiding place. "So bloody," he said.

"Yeah, so what? Now shake yourself and lead that express wagon over to the trees where we got our rig. Hurry, you worthless lump! We ain't got forever."

Avery did as instructed, but he kept repeating over and over, "So bloody, so bloody."

CHAPTER 17

Maguire's Opera House had been playing to packed houses ever since it opened in Virginia City some months earlier. Anticipation was running high for the coming attraction *Mazeppa*. Lurid handbills depicted scantily-clad actress Adah Isaacs Menken bound to the back of a fiercely snorting runaway stallion. It caught the boys' attention. Each one imagined himself as her rescuer, a modern-day knight-errant, dispatching villains with six-gun instead of sword.

The boys liked drinking and gambling as recreations, but they liked variety, too. A pretty actress and an opening night provided just the different kind of excitement they craved. Even though Belle Boyd did not have the reputation or the promotion of "The Menken," her soft-spoken, helpless femininity inspired the boys to chivalrous thoughts. This was especially true since the advertised production was *Fortune's Handmaid*, a riches-to-rags-to-riches story with despicable, thieving relations and a much-abused, pure-hearted heroine.

Maguire's was filled to capacity. From the orchestra pit to the billiard tables in the foyer, it was crowded with mine superintendents wearing diamond stickpins and miners wearing their only clean shirts.

Lijah Stone was holding court in one of the red-velvet-lined boxes in the second tier of private rooms. Without giving specifics, he was bragging about having evened a score. Stone was secure in the belief that even when the double murder came to light and people began to speculate, old Clay would be too terrified to ever act as a witness against him. The proof of the accuracy of his belief was the fact that while the town had already heard of the wreck on the previous day of the Gould and Curry lift, it was being referred to as an accident. Stone figured that the bodies had not yet been found and that Clay was keeping quiet.

The opening notes from the orchestra hurried the late arrivals into their seats and urged the last-minute drinkers to leave the ivory-inlaid mahogany bar. Lijah Stone and his cronies settled back in the gilt chairs as the house-lights reflected in the crystal chandeliers began to dim.

A spotlight aimed from the catwalk overhead was directed toward the center of the still-closed curtain. It illuminated a beautiful painted backdrop of sparkling Lake Tahoe surrounded by an evergreen forest.

There was only a moment to admire the painting, then the curtain was raised. The opening scene showed the interior of a mansion's great hall and a beautiful woman caring for an invalid father.

There was a disturbance at the front of the theater. A late-comer made his way down the aisle of the theater. He probably would not have attracted Lijah's attention except for the fact that he came all the way down front. The front row of seats was reserved for the drama critics and other reporters of the *Enterprise* and the *Union* and the *Gold Hill News*. This tardy playgoer walked into the ranks of newspapermen, and singled one out for a greeting. That man stood and started up the aisle in a hurry. His characteristic shuffle was gone, but there was no mistaking his face.

Stone leaned over the railing and stared. It could not be, but it was! Somehow Sam Clemens had escaped from the mine shaft. And if *he* had, then perhaps . . . Stone half rose from his chair and turned to find himself staring into the barrel of Tom Dawson's Navy Thirty-Six.

"Stone," Tom said softly, "some folks want to talk to you about a little mining accident." He gestured over his shoulder toward three grim-faced Gould and Curry security guards.

"Why me?" blustered Stone. Heads in the audience swivelled to look up at the box. Then Stone saw the bandaged head and fiercely cold eyes of Clay, the hoist operator.

"Attacking a woman one day and a mining operation the next," said Tom, shaking his head. "Seems to me you managed to get everybody in the Comstock down on you this time."

Stone started to protest, then noticed all his former friends melting away and disappearing through the curtained exit behind the guards. "Here now," he said, extending his hands in front of him. "I'll come peaceable."

Everyone was so eager to see that Stone kept his hands empty and in plain sight that no one paid any attention to his feet. With the toe of one boot underneath the velvet-cushioned chair, Stone smacked it sharply upward, flipping the chair into Tom's face.

Tom fought to knock the chair aside without accidentally firing his Colt, for fear of hitting a bystander. Stone had no such compunction. As soon as the furniture was airborne, he went for his gun.

The first shot hit an oaken chair leg, which deflected it just enough to make the bullet miss hitting Tom in the chest and smash a brass lamp instead. The guards scattered and several women in the audience screamed.

Firing again, Stone jumped toward the painted wooden railing that marked the front edge of the theater box. This second shot was not aimed at all and crashed harmlessly into the ceiling, but it made half the theatergoers hug the legs of their chairs, while the other half drew weapons of their own.

The drop to the Opera House floor was fifteen feet, but Stone vaulted the rail without a moment's thought. He smashed, boots first, into a recently vacated chair, splintering it into myriads of pieces and sending another wave of screams through the audience.

On stage, the invalid father experienced a remarkable healing, jumped up from his sickbed and ran with his daughter into the wings. As they were running out of the spotlight, producer Maguire ran into it. With both arms raised, he pleaded for calm. "Please, please!" he begged. "No more shooting! Settle your differences somewheres else!"

Stone came up from the floor with the seat of the broken chair tangled around one leg, but with his pistol still in his hand. He knocked aside a fiddle player, then hoisted himself up onto the stage. "Give it up!" Tom yelled over the hubbub of shouts and cries. "You can't get away."

The only reply Stone made was to fire another awkwardly off-balance shot toward Tom. This third slug clipped a crystal chandelier and sent it plummeting toward the crowd, who clawed all over one another to escape its crushing impact. For an instant, everyone's attention was distracted and Stone ran offstage into the wings where Belle had taken refuge.

"Not that way," she hissed, as Stone made for the stage door. "Up to the catwalk and out on the roof."

The audience on the floor of the theater could not see where Stone had gone. They guessed that he would exit by the stage door and a large crowd of men brandishing guns surged out the rear of the auditorium along with the guards who had been with Tom.

From Tom's position up in the box, he could see Stone pause halfway up the ladder to thrust his pistol into his waistband. Glancing upward toward the catwalk, Tom spotted Stone's goal: large windows set into the ceiling above the narrow iron ledge that provided ventilation for the hot lights. If Stone reached them, he could escape onto the roof of the Opera House and, in the darkness of the surrounding shops and stores, make good his escape.

"He's headed for the catwalk," Tom shouted. "After him! He's trying for the roof!" But no one heard him amid all the other noise and confusion, and Tom's warning went unheeded.

The unarmed spotlight operator saw Stone coming up the ladder and ran for his life. The man pushed open one of the large windows and took himself out of harm's way.

There was one chance for Tom to head off Lijah Stone. Along the corridor of the second story boxes were French doors that opened out onto a balcony. Tom threw open the closest one and jumped through to stand on the overhang. A drainpipe provided a means of ascent to the roof and the row of rooftop windows through which Stone would be coming.

Tom pulled himself onto the roof not an instant too soon. The dark mass of a man's body appeared, framed in the open window as Stone stood on the iron railing of the catwalk. "Hold it right there, Stone," Tom demanded.

In response, a surprised Lijah Stone drew his pistol at the same moment that his boot heel slipped on the slick iron rail of the catwalk. His hand flew up and the pistol struck the window and was knocked from his grasp. It spun away from him and dropped to the theater floor.

"Come on out, Stone," Tom instructed, gesturing with his Navy.

"Come in and get me," Stone retorted, then jumped from the railing back down to the catwalk's iron grate. He turned to run back toward the ladder.

Diving in the window right after him, Tom landed on Stone's back and knocked him down on the narrow hanging ledge. The two men grappled on the walkway, each struggling for control of Tom's pistol. Tom tried to turn the muzzle toward Stone to call a halt to the battle, but Stone smashed Tom's hand down again and again on the sharp metal lip of the catwalk's floor.

Feeling his grip weakening as his hand numbed, Tom pounded Stone in the kidneys with his left. In return he caught a headbutt that opened a gash above his left eye. Fearing that Stone might get the pistol, Tom deliberately let it fly from his hand and off the catwalk the next time his wrist was pounded on the metal.

Stone gave an angry, frustrated bellow. He locked his hands together and brought them down hard toward

Tom's face. Tom jerked aside and the blow thudded into the iron grate.

Sitting upright to give himself more force, Stone tried again to land a piledriver on Tom's head. It was a blow intended to crush his opponent's skull like an eggshell.

Using the force of Lijah Stone's downward swing to aid him, Tom kicked up hard in an attempt to roll Stone over his head. Stone tried to keep from being thrown off by stopping the swing of his arms and flattening out his body as Tom pushed him over. Instead of rolling off Tom onto the catwalk, Lijah Stone sailed through the opening between the narrow iron rails and plummeted forty feet to the Opera House floor.

There were a few people who remained in the auditorium. They heard the noise overhead and watched the fight on the catwalk, dodging the falling pistols. A collective intake of breath went up when Stone jackknifed through the bars. When he landed with a dull thud in one of the aisles, there was a momentary silence, followed by a clamor of exclamations and questions.

His face streaming blood, Tom held a bandanna pressed over the wound for a moment before tying it around his head. He walked unsteadily to the ladder that led down to the stage and slowly descended it. Partway down he had to stop and squeeze his eyes shut till a wave of dizziness passed.

A few moments later, Tom stood over the crumpled form of Lijah Stone. He was not dead, but nearly so. "Get a doctor," Tom called to the people who stood milling around. "Get a doctor!" he said again with exasperation.

"No . . . time," groaned Lijah Stone. "Get preacher,

'stead. Quick!" He bit off the words in a spasm of agony. "Get Bollin . . . nobody else!"

Tom looked to see that someone was going to get the pastor, then sat down and stared at the wreck of a man. A wasted life, now in terror of his soul's unreadiness. One of Stone's eyes darted toward Tom, took in his presence. The other already seemed fixed and vacant.

"Want to tell you, Dawson—" Stone began.

Tom started. Stone had used Tom's real name. *His identity was known!*

"They are on to you . . . hired me to kill you . . ."

Tom nodded his understanding. "Then you're the one who fired through the floor of the hotel and caused the wagon accident?"

Stone's face contorted in a mixture of agony and confusion. "No," he said with difficulty. "Don't know what you mean. . . . They came to me after our fight . . ."

"Who?" Tom asked. "Who came to you?"

"Don't know names," Stone's head lolled to one side when he tried to shake it, then it would not straighten up again. "Get . . . get preacher!" he said with urgency.

"All right, Stone, lie quiet. I'm sure he's on the way."

"Good." Stone's word came with a long, drawn-out sigh, then his body arched again in a spasm of pain. "Dawson!" he almost shouted. "Girl . . . the actress . . . She's one of 'em."

"I know," said Tom quietly.

Pastor Bollin was hustled through the doors of the Opera House. He came and knelt beside Stone. The killer's eye flickered on Bollin's features and one corner of his mouth twitched in a smile. "Knew you'd . . . come.

163

Best man I . . . ever saw. Don't mind losing . . . to better men." Stone's breath was shallow and a pink froth appeared on his lips. "Help me, preacher . . . Ah God, I'm so scared."

Tom stood, and moving all the curious onlookers before him with the force of an expression that accepted no argument, cleared the great hall. At the last he looked over his shoulder to see Pastor Bollin bent to speak in Lijah Stone's ear and the dying man's attempt to nod.

Sam met Tom on the steps outside Maguire's. "You all right?" he asked, looking with concern at the clotted blood drying on Tom's face and the gory bandanna.

"Stone's dead," Tom said. "He tried to escape and fell from the catwalk. Where'd you go, anyway?"

"Message came right before things heated up at the Opera House. Bullion shipment was robbed 'tween here and Tahoe. Only one guard escaped alive."

"That's it, then," concluded Tom. "I'm sure of it. They put Stone up to finishing me off while they went after the silver. How much did they get?"

"Twenty or thirty thousand. Oh, and there's more. Soon as the word came in, a reporter tried to meet the mine superintendent, a man named Baldwin. Seems he lit a shuck out of here earlier today. What do you make of that?"

"Same as you. He must have had a hand in the robbery. Posse out after him?"

"And the Army," Sam amended. "Some reporter for the *Enterprise* tipped off the soldiers that this was a secesh plot." Sam looked very pleased with himself.

"Well, round up some more men," Tom instructed.

"What for? Who's left to arrest?"

"Belle Boyd."

"The actress?" Sam asked with surprise. "What's she got to do with this?"

"She's in it up to her pretty neck," said Tom grimly. "But on my word, she's about to get helpful."

CHAPTER 18

Reynolds, Perry, Hastings, Ingram, and Law gathered aboard the *Chapman*. The recently stolen silver shipment had already been exchanged for weapons through a Mexican arms dealer who asked no questions.

"Five cases of powder," Perry read from a list. "One hundred fifty revolvers, thirty rifles, one hundred fifty pounds of bullets, two hundred cannon shells and," he paused impressively, "two brass twelve pounders, brought aboard in crates labelled 'machinery.'"

"Well done," complimented Reynolds, "and again to you, Ingram and Hastings."

"I still want to know when the thousand-man army will show up," growled Law.

"Hold your tongue," snapped Perry. "Just let us seize one Pacific mail steamer and the take won't be thirty thousand dollars, it'll be three hundred thousand or even three million. Men will flock to our recruiting."

"Maybe," said Law without enthusiasm. "One passage at a time I says. Where's my next payment?"

Reynolds handed it over grudgingly. "See that you earn that," he demanded.

"Aye," agreed Law. "Reckon I will day after tomorrow."

"Are you certain, Ingram, that Dawson is disposed of?" Perry asked.

"Nothing easier," said Ingram. "Stone told us that the spy and a newspaper snoop were both at the bottom of a thousand-foot shaft."

Tom shook hands with Sam and prepared to board the Pioneer Stage for what he hoped would be the fastest possible trip back to Frisco. He had stepped one foot up on the coach when Belle Boyd was led out of the Express Line office in handcuffs. "Just a minute," he called to the driver, and he moved in front of the procession leading Belle to jail.

"You can only have a minute, Mr. Dawson," said the Express Lines guard in charge. "We've lost two good men and thirty thousand in bullion. This little she-devil don't even try to act innocent. She's been spoutin' venom about Abe Lincoln and everybody else since we caught her. The big bosses want her locked up pronto an' us to hit the trail after Superintendent Baldwin."

"I won't tell you anything, Mr. Wilson or Dawson— whatever your name is," Belle spat at Tom.

"Belle," Tom said reasonably, "the game is up. You're already an accessory in two murders. Tell me what you know before your gang gets you involved in more."

Belle smiled a malicious smile. "Here's all I'll tell you: You won't see that little black brat ever again!"

The audience chamber was especially tense. Two ranks

of boo-how-doys stood attentively in front of Fujing Toy's throne. Each carried a hatchet at shoulder arms and appeared ready to use it.

The reason for the special precaution was the arrival of an emissary of the most powerful rival tong, the Sue Yops. It was not impossible to think that this ambassador might have orders to assassinate Fujing. The show of force was to impress on the visitor how immediate and horrible would be the vengeance if any such attack were attempted.

The emissary announced that he had come bearing a gift from the Sue Yop leader to Fujing Toy. Before he approached any closer, two blackshirts stepped forward, and at his permission, the ambassador allowed himself to be searched. He was in his best formal attire, wrapped in yards of silk that rustled continuously. The ambassador advanced on his knees with the parcel, also wrapped in rustling silk, and placed it at Fujing's feet.

A snap of the fingers summoned Mont. He placed his peacock fan in a brass holder and crept forward on his stomach as he had been taught.

Loops of bright yellow ribbon tied up the lid of the box. Mont carefully untied the bands, then looked to see if Fujing wished him to open the present further. A frown of the impassive face told him that Mont should only pass the box up to the Tong lord's lap.

Mont was still kneeling at Fujing's feet when with a final rattle and rustle of the silk wrapping, the Sum Yop master thrust his hand into the box. A terrible scream erupted from his mouth, and he flung himself backward and the box away. The rattlesnake that had been coiled inside the gift had attached itself to Fujing's forearm by its fangs.

The ambassador-assassin grabbed the fallen box and from inside the thickly padded interior drew a pistol. Fujing was still screaming and shaking his arm frantically, trying to dislodge the snake. Its fangs had pierced the brocade of his sleeve as well as his flesh and it continued to hang there.

Two of the blackshirts went down in quick succession to shots from the emissary's pistol, then there was a crash against the entry door and armed men burst in. These were also dressed in black, but they wore yellow armbands and carried two-pronged pitchforks instead of hatchets.

Fujing had finally succeeded in shaking the snake loose. It fell across Mont's back where he cowered at the foot of the throne. The rattlesnake slithered onto the floor of the platform and quickly retreated under the throne where it coiled and struck out at the air.

Reacting swiftly to the invading Sue Yops, Han picked up a solid oak table that was almost eight feet long. He turned it into a combination shield and battering ram, carrying the front rank of the enemy soldiers back through the door.

Suddenly he stopped and flung down the piece of furniture. Ripping a leg the size of a fencepost off the table, he set out across the throne room, scattering startled musicians, fearful guests, and confused bodyguards in all directions.

When a blackshirt sized him up as a traitor and took a swing with a hatchet, Han parried the chop with the improvised quarter-staff. He then spun the end around so that it caught the man under the chin and lifted him completely off the floor with its impact.

The assassin had killed two more of Fujing's men before their hatchets had silenced him, and now several waves of yellow armbands flooded through the doorway. Every boo-how-doy was engaged in fighting for his life, and no one had any time to regard Han, except when he grabbed two opposing bodyguards and smashed both their heads together before leaping over them.

The dread master of the Sum Yop Tong had fallen off of his throne. He had fainted and his unconscious form lay on top of Mont.

Picking up his recent owner as if he were a fragment of lint to be brushed away, Han flicked Fujing against the wall. Then gathering up Mont by a handful of robe, Han made a hasty exit up the passage behind the throne.

"You all right?" he asked Mont when he had ceased swinging the boy like a dinner pail and brought him up head high.

"Yes," Mont coughed. "Just a little shook up is all. Does you know your way out of here?"

The giant man shook his head.

Mont thought for a moment. "Can you get us back to the main corridor?"

"Yes," Han replied. "This I do."

"All right, then," Mont concluded. "I'll show us the way out."

"Oh no," worried Mont as he and Han stood in front of the iron gate that covered the passageway behind the opium den. "It's locked!"

Han rattled the grill with one hand. "So it is," he said.

The fleeing pair had traveled fast, but the news of the great battle raging between the rival tongs seemed to have traveled even faster. All the usual traffic in the underground tunnels had suddenly disappeared. The normal commerce of the common Chinese folk would resume as soon as it was safe, and it mattered little to them which master won.

Han and Mont had needed to hide only once on their flight to the iron gate. But as soon as the group of yellow armbands raced by, the two continued their escape and now stood before the locked gate.

"So it is," Han said again, giving the gate another shake. He set Mont down a few paces behind him and off to the side. "Wait," he said simply.

Curling his fingers around the latticework, Han bent his back like an ox leaning into a heavy load. There was a moment of immobility, and then a rending sound as chunks of bricks and mortar fell from the gate's anchor bolts. The entire gate and its frame pulled free of the wall, and Han threw it aside with a crash.

When they at last emerged into the alley off Washington, it was late at night. "Good thing," Mont observed, looking down at his own fanciful robes and up at the imposing height of his friend. "We two is gonna stand out like . . . like I don't know what!"

"Where we go now, little friend?"

"Well, now, we . . . that is I . . ." Mont paused and considered. "I don't rightly know. We can't go back to the hotel 'count a dem bad fellers might still be there, an' I don't know if Tom is back."

"If we seek your home?" Han asked.

"Greenville? It's a powerful far piece from here. I think de best thing to do is to put some miles 'tween us an' Frisco. How 'bout we cross the bay by steamer and figger the rest out tomorrow?"

Han agreed and the two were soon slipping through alleys on their way to the wharfs. They had just turned the last corner before the waterfront when they heard the voices of several men approaching.

By much folding of knees and tucking in of elbows, it was just barely possible for Han to conceal himself behind a packing crate. Mont peeped around to examine the passersby who stood together in a little huddled cluster beneath a street lamp. "It's them!" Mont exclaimed in a stifled whisper. "The pointy bearded one and the Army man! And with 'em is . . . the one I saw in Richmond!"

"It a blessing, then, that we see first," Han said. "Come, we slip back quickly."

"No, wait," Mont insisted. "I got's to see where they go. This is what I come all this way for."

The men walked toward a small sailing ship docked at the wharf. They all descended below-decks on the schooner, leaving a hatch cover half-open, from which a lantern light glowed. "Come on," urged Mont. "Let's get closer. I gotta hear what they says."

Without waiting for Han's approval, Mont darted across the intervening space and crept up on the deck. Han followed and plucked at Mont's sleeve with huge but gentle fingers, wanting the boy to come away.

Instead, Mont put a warning finger to his lips and bent his ear to the hatch cover.

"Is everything on board?" a voice asked.

"Loaded and stowed," answered another. "The twelve pounders can be rigged out in five minutes."

"When do the recruits get here?"

"First light. Then we can get underway. Where are Ingram and Law?"

"Coming," a younger voice replied. "Should be here any minute now."

Mont shot a worried look at Han and they started to creep back toward the gangplank. The sound of heavy footsteps clumping along the dock sent them scurrying aft. Han had to lie down flat on the deck to fit behind the boom and furled sail of the mizzenmast.

Reynolds greeted Ingram on the deck. "All the officers are here except Law," Mont heard him say. "I'm going back before I'm missed. Get underway as soon as you can after the crew arrives."

CHAPTER 19

Waking with a start, Tom had a moment's difficulty in placing his whereabouts. Dimmed lanterns casting a glow over tufted velvet cushions and a steady drumming sound served as reminders that he was in the forward passenger salon of the steamer *Yosemite*. Thirty-six hours of churning stage and steamer travel had given him plenty of time to ponder questions but produced few answers.

Had Belle been telling the truth about Mont? Were the

secesh holding him as a hostage, or had something worse happened to his little friend? Tom not only did not know the answer, he could not figure out how to easily determine it. As far as the gang knew, Tom reasoned, only two people in San Francisco knew that Wilson was really Dawson: the gruff, unhelpful Commander Fry and the obliging Lieutenant Reynolds.

Suddenly, Tom realized one of the two had to be a traitor. Either would be in a position to assist the Confederacy in a scheme that involved piracy and seizing of forts and arsenals. Perhaps both men were conspiring against the Union? How was he to tell? If Reynolds was a traitor, then Tom had delivered Mont right into the gang's hands. Then again, maybe Mont was really safe at Fort Point—but now he must find out without revealing himself, or risking Mont's life.

One other troubling question remained: What about the other attempts on Tom's life? Was there an unknown member of the conspiracy who had been stalking Tom? But how could the others not already know?

Tom went outside to stand all alone on the fog-shrouded foredeck. He listened to the mournful sound of the fog whistles and hoped that the chill swirling air would clear his head.

Mont and Han stayed concealed behind the sail, hoping for a chance to somehow get off the *Chapman*. Each time they made a move toward the gangplank, another small group of men would arrive out of the darkness and send them scuttling back to their hiding place.

Toward dawn, Mont had actually fallen asleep in a fold

of the furled sails while Han kept watch. A sharp poke in the boy's ribs with a twice-normal length finger woke him. "What is it?" he asked sleepily.

"Shh," Han cautioned. "Men talk louder now."

It was true. The quiet rocking of the ship and the gentle lapping of the waves against the side were disturbed by the sound of voices arguing. "He's not coming, I tell you! He's sold us out!" worried one.

"Then let's sail right now," said another.

"We can't none of us navigate. We'll sink for sure!"

"Do you want to rot in a Federal prison instead?"

The clamor rose even louder, with some voices calling to cast off at once while others argued that the enterprise should be abandoned altogether. The somewhat shrill voice of Jasper Perry climbed above the rest, from the steps of the companionway, "Nobody is going anywhere! This Colt and I will see to that. We'll stay here, quiet," he underlined with his tone, "till full light. If Law hasn't shown by then, we'll sail without him. You all know too much to leave now! Is that clear?"

A grumbling murmur of assent answered him, but Mont and Han had not stayed to hear it. Fearful that the crew were coming up on deck, they slipped down a small aft hatch that led down into the evil-smelling darkness of the ship's bilge.

There they waited and prayed.

Yosemite's forward flagstaff carried the sky-blue triangular pennant of the California Steam Navigation Company. Tom glanced up at it, then back to the gray water streaming past the broad prow of the ship. He shivered slightly in the chill and wished he'd put on his jacket before coming on deck. *How much longer?* he wondered. *Can't this thing go any faster?*

Tom put his hand up to lean against the flagstaff, when a furtive tread behind him made him turn. As he did, a gun barrel slammed into the side of his head and a boot in his back tried to shove him into the bay.

Spinning half around on the pole, Tom crouched on the deck and found himself staring into the business end of a forty-four Remington. Raising his eyes upward from the gun, he took in a form bundled in a thick blanket coat with the collar turned up. Next he saw an enormous moustache, and behind it the cold, intent face of Michael Pettibone. "Pettibone! So, it was you all along!"

"Keep your voice down, Tom," the deputy ordered. "I didn't aim to shoot you, but if you yell I won't have a choice."

"But you were going to toss me in the bay. Why, Mike?"

Pettibone shrugged. "The Golden Circle paid me to keep quiet about some holdups, that's all. And everything was quiet, too, till you decided to stir things up again. I kept hoping I could scare you into giving up and going home. But it's too late for that now and—"

"And now you've got to kill me, is that it?"

"'Fraid so, Tom," Pettibone agreed, gesturing with the pistol for Tom to stand. Tom studied the distance to the deputy, knowing that he'd have to spring into the blast of the gun. Pettibone's finger tightened on the trigger. *That's it,* Tom thought. *He's waiting for the next time the fog whistle blows.*

Tom sprang, and at that exact second the whistle sounded. Not the hooting noise of the fog signal, but the long, drawn-out scream of the collision alarm. *Yosemite* swung sharply to starboard and heeled over with the momentum of the turn. Tom's lunge connected with the pistol just as it fired, the bullet striking the deck between his feet.

A shuddering crash made the steamer tremble all over like a wet dog shaking himself dry. The unexpected impact threw Tom and the deputy spinning toward the rail and over it into the icy waters below.

Striking the surface flung the two men apart. Pettibone floundered in the heavy coat he wore, struggling frantically, before slipping beneath the waves. The current carried Tom along the side of the steamer. He fought to keep his head above water, gasping for air, unable to call out for help and alarmed at the numbness already overtaking his arms and legs.

A round tower loomed out of the fog, like a giant floating tin can. *I must be dying,* Tom thought. *I'm seeing things.*

His hands struck hard metal and scrabbled at a deck that looked like an iron-plated raft. The next instant, strong arms were lifting him out of the water. Two bearded sailors snapped to attention as an officer strode up and demanded, "What's the damage? This cursed fog and *Camanche*'s profile so low in the water, too. I . . . Dawson, is that you?"

Through chattering teeth, Tom assured Commander Fry that it was indeed. "But what is this?" he asked as he was wrapped in a blanket and helped below.

"This," Fry announced proudly, "is our new ironclad, *Camanche*. She's out for sea trials today under cover of darkness, but I suppose our secret's out now. Gordon," he called to one of the sailors, "what's the damage?"

"None to us, sir," was the report, "and minor to *Yosemite*. She's steaming away right enough. Glancing blow only. She struck us."

"Good thing it wasn't the other way round," Fry harrumphed. "Our ram would have ripped her belly out."

"Commander," Tom said urgently, "the secesh plotters have seized a bullion shipment and are arming a ship— perhaps have already done so. What's more, I think Lieutenant Reynolds at Fort Point may be one of them."

"Old news, that," commented Fry. "Reynolds was arrested last night. Seems Captain Tompkins wasn't just ill; he was poisoned, but lived. What's this about a ship?"

"The *Chapman*, sir. The plot is to outfit her as a privateer."

"*Chapman*, eh? I know where she's berthed. We'll steam over there now and take a look."

"One more thing," asked Tom, looking back at the departing bulk of the *Yosemite* and the receding line of foaming water where Pettibone sank. "Has anyone seen the black child, Mont James?"

CHAPTER 20

"Hey, Han," Mont whispered. "What are all those noises?" The *Chapman*'s hold had been as quiet as a tomb. Now the sound of running feet could be heard along with shouted commands and a creaking, sighing commentary from the ship herself.

"Very bad," observed Han, holding Mont close. "Ship making sail—leaving dock."

"Come on, then," Mont exclaimed, struggling free. "We've got to get off!"

Mont started up the ladder when an arm as long as he was tall reached out a hand to grasp his ankle and draw him back. "I will go first," Han said. He picked Mont up and set him on a cold coil of rusty anchor chain.

"There's the *Chapman* now," said Fry, pointing, "and she's already underway. Helmsman," he ordered, "steer to cross her bow." *Camanche* turned to intercept the schooner, whose sails were hoisted and filling with the rising morning breeze.

At a distance of three hundred yards, there was a flash from the *Chapman*, a splash nearby *Camanche*, and then the report of a cannon. "Shelling us, by thunder," commented Fry. "Foolish move. No doubt of their intentions now."

"Why don't we fire back?" asked Tom.

"Can't," answered the officer, indicating the empty gun carriages inside the revolving turret over their heads, where *Camanche*'s cannons would go. "She's not armed yet. This was only supposed to be a sea trial, not a combat patrol."

Another flash aboard *Chapman*, and a shell smashed into the ironclad's deck. There was a loud clanging noise and some exclamations of alarm from below deck, but no damage done.

"More speed," Fry ordered. "If she gets the wind of us, she can outrun us."

Camanche's vibrations increased as more steam pressure was applied to turn the propeller, but the *Chapman* was still pulling away. "She's making to round Alcatraz on this leg, then turn downwind for the run down the channel," Fry observed.

"We can't let them get away," Tom said anxiously. "Can't we stop her?"

"Not without a miracle," Fry replied. "She's got her speed up now. There's no way we can catch her."

The hatch cover slid back noiselessly. *Chapman*'s deck stretched forward of the small opening, with the men on deck grouped around the twelve-pound cannons, or tensely holding rifles. They were arguing and pointing, angry and afraid.

Han slipped up the ladder. The closest sailor was the helmsman, who was alternately looking up at the sails, out toward the approaching *Camanche*, and ahead to the dim outline of the rock of Alcatraz.

For Han, the distance to the helm station was only two strides. There was not even a startled exclamation from the sailor when two fists the size of melons struck him on both sides of his head at once. The man fell in a crumpled heap, and Han peered anxiously around for a small boat in which he and Mont could escape.

The helm, untended, spun lazily off course. The sails flapped and *Chapman* began to lose speed. The men on deck did not seem to notice as they clumsily loaded and fired the cannon, with Jasper Perry maintaining order at the point of a gun.

"We're gaining," Tom observed.

"Yes," agreed Commander Fry as bullets began to rattle and ricochet off *Camanche*'s iron hide. "We're inside small arms range now. Helmsman," he ordered, "I'll have that ship rammed, if you please." To a knot of sailors gathered below, he said, "Mr. O'Toole, have the men prepared to board that vessel and seize it."

"Helmsman!" shouted Perry, finally noticing *Chapman*'s decreasing speed and wandering course. "You at the wheel, where are you steering? Who is that?" he yelled, catching sight of Han's looming figure.

"Rush him, whoever he is!" shouted Ingram. "Shoot him down."

Han seized a fire ax and in one swing chopped the main sheet in two, dropping the sail, and spoiling the aim of the confused mass of men up forward. He then severed the line that restrained the boom of the mizzenmast. With a huge shove, he swept the boom up the length of the schooner, catching the knot of men who were advancing on him, carrying eight men over the side, and crushing the others against the rail and into one another.

"Brace yourself," Fry called below. "Prepare to ram!"

Camanche's broad iron wedge plunged into the *Chapman* amidships. With a splintering roar as if a thousand trees were felled at once, *Camanche*'s ram ripped into the schooner, tumbling the secesh sailors about the deck like marbles.

"Stand to the guns!" Perry roared as men began raising their hands in surrender.

"Stand and fight!" yelled Ingram as he leveled his pistol at Tom and the sailors swarming out of *Camanche*'s hold.

From the rear deck of the *Chapman*, a hundred pounds of chain came whirling through the air like a runaway saw blade. It struck Perry and Ingram as they stood beside the cannon and wrapped completely around them both, binding them together in an iron embrace. There was just time for each to vent a horrified scream directly into the other's face, before the weight of the chain carried them over the side and out of sight into the depths of San Francisco Bay. All the others threw down their weapons, and begged to surrender.

Tom vaulted over from the deck of the ironclad to the steeply listing *Chapman*. Out of the fearful, clamoring men on board, he selected Avery Hastings and demanded, "Where is Mont James? Where is the black child? Talk quick or I'll throw you in after your friends."

"I swear I don't know," pleaded Avery. "Don't kill me, and call off your Chinese giant. He's a madman!" He looked nervously at Han, who loomed overhead with a menace.

"My giant?" asked Tom.

"Hey!" said a small voice from the stern hatch. "I wants out of here!"

Han leaned over the opening and reached his arm in like a cargo crane lowering its hook. Out of the hold and into the brightening sunshine rode a laughing and smiling Mont James.

The front room at the Dawson home was buzzing with eager questions for Mont and Tom from Emily, Nathan, Jed and Colonel Mason. "You mean that Pettibone poisoned our horse and then came back here the next day?" Emily shuddered.

"Yes," Tom agreed, "but only because he didn't know that Mont and I had already left. He was trying to frighten us out of going."

"It certainly frightened *us*," Emily said.

"Twice more in Virginia City he tried again, each time a little more murderously," Tom added, without going into detail. "The funny thing is, none of the *Chapman* conspirators knew him to give away his guilty secrets, so he was really running from shadows."

Emily nodded. "The wicked flee when no one is pursuing," she said.

"Sometimes the innocent do a heap of fleeing, too; right, Mont?"

The boy bobbed his head vigorously.

"Was you really in a Chinese opium den?" asked Jed. "I seen pictures of them in the Police Gazette."

"Saw them," Emily corrected, "and I'll not have you reading that trashy magazine. The very idea!"

"No'm," Jed said, hastily redirecting the conversation. "What about this Hand feller, Mont? Is he really seven feet tall?"

"Han," corrected Mont, "an' he look ten feet tall to me!"

"What happened to him, Tom?" Emily asked.

"With his share of the reward money for helping to recover the silver shipment, he could afford to go home to China and live like a king," Tom explained. "But he bought eighteen others out of slavery and hired 'em on to run a laundry! What I still wonder," Tom continued, "is what panicked the gang into sailing so abruptly?"

"Seems I get to answer one," said Colonel Mason, laughing. "They thought that their hired captain turned traitor, but Law never sold them out after all. He was discovered two days later in his hotel room, stinking drunk."

Emily asked, "And what about the army traitor?"

"He will probably hang, ma'am," said Mason.

"I see," said Emily. "And the man Mont saw way back in Richmond; that one glimpse that started this whole chase? He seems very young and more misguided than evil. What will happen to him?"

Tom and Colonel Mason exchanged grins, and then Tom answered, "Seems that the *Chapman* was piloted correctly after all, and that brief voyage took Hastings exactly where he belonged. He will be staying for quite some time as a guest of the Union army . . . at the military prison on Alcatraz."

"And will you be 'staying for quite some time' with us, Tom?" asked Emily with a sudden change of tone that stopped Dawson's revelry in its tracks. The silence that followed had Tom searching for an answer.

"It's good to be . . . home, Emily," Tom said. His tone matched hers, and their eyes met. Neither looked away.

"It wasn't quite home without you," Emily spoke through shining eyes.

Only Colonel Mason had noticed what was *really* being said, but Tom knew that Jed would figure it out if they kept this conversation going. "Sounds like we've got a lot to talk about, Em—*later!*"

Center Point Publishing
600 Brooks Road • PO Box 1
Thorndike ME 04986-0001 USA

(207) 568-3717

US & Canada:
1 800 929-9108